the Reveal

Becoming Beka Book 4

the Reveal

Sarah Anne Sumpolec

MOODY PUBLISHERS
CHICAGO

© 2005 by
Sarah Anne Sumpolec

Beka's song, "You Found Me," is copyrighted by Andy Jones. Used by permission.

Library of Congress Cataloging-in-Publication Data

Sumpolec, Sarah Anne.
   The reveal / Sarah Anne Sumpolec.
     p. cm. — (Becoming Beka ; bk. 4)
   Summary: As she enters her senior year of high school, Beka continues to explore her relationship with God by taking a mission trip to Haiti and helping a former enemy who has attempted suicide.
   ISBN-13: 978-0-8024-6454-5
   [1. Suicide—Fiction. 2. High schools—Fiction. 3. Schools—Fiction. 4. Haiti—Fiction. 5. Christian life—Fiction.] I. Title.

PZ7.R9563Re 2005
[Fic]—dc22

2004028016

ISBN: 0-8024-6454-8
ISBN-13: 978-0-8024-6454-5

1 3 5 7 9 10 8 6 4 2

Printed in the United States of America

For Cassie—
you are a joy and a delight.

ACKNOWLEDGMENTS

First, I want to thank all my wonderful readers who have continued on this journey with Beka. You all are why I write. I appreciate each one of you.

As always, a special thanks to the team at Moody: Andy McGuire, for believing in Beka and me; Cheryl Dunlop, for her editing skills; and Barb Fisher, for her fabulous covers—aren't they great? Thanks also must go to Janet Kobobel Grant, my ever-patient agent.

I am certain I have the most wonderful little family on earth—and definitely the most amazing husband. Without his support and encouragement, I would have grown weary long ago. My three little girls, Molly, Cassie, and Lydia, are a blessing each and every day, and

I know how blessed I am to have the chance to be home with them and, at the same time, write down Beka's journey for all of you.

I am also grateful for the skills and talent of my friend Andy Jones, whose real song has become Beka's song, and to Jeni Bradshaw, whose unique gift has given Beka a voice of her own. Thank you for sharing your talents! I also am so appreciative of Mary Custalow, my faithful first reader, and of my devoted friend Dona Wilson, who keeps me grounded with her friendship.

And last, but most definitely not least, my heart gives thanks to Jesus Christ. In Him I live and move and have my being. May Your name be praised.

I think I made a huge mistake," I said, slumping into the molded blue plastic chair. "I don't think I can do it."

"You were excited about going just yesterday," Lori said. She parked my small suitcase and sat down next to me.

"I know." I watched the rest of the team counting bags and talking in little clusters. There were twenty-three of us, but I didn't know most of them very well at all. And here I was about to fly with all of them to a third-world country. What was I thinking?

I spotted Josh crouching by a group of bags. *That's* what I had been thinking. Spending just ten more days with Josh before he disappeared across the country to go to college was most of the reason I was now sitting in an airport about to say good-bye to my dad and my best friend. A wave of fear hit me as the bustle around me seemed to move in slow motion. *What if the plane crashes? What if I get one of those freaky diseases they told us about? What if . . .*

"Beka!" Lori snapped her fingers near my nose.

"What?"

Lori shook her head. "Once again. You really think it's a mistake?"

"Maybe." I waved my hand toward the group. "They all seem to have some big, noble purpose for going. What am I doing here?"

Lori smiled. "Josh talked you into going. I'm sure he'll take care of you."

I turned and scowled at her. She laughed.

"All I'm saying is, go, enjoy yourself. Don't worry about what got you here; just go do it. Let's go. Your dad's waving at you."

I looked where Lori was pointing and saw my dad looking a little frantic. He was standing behind a mountain of suitcases and other baggage. Lori stood up, and I forced myself to get up, still considering how I could change my mind. I just wasn't ready. The trip had been postponed and then reinstated. I had already decided I couldn't have gone in September. I would have missed school, and Josh would have already left for Seattle Pacific. But when they suddenly rescheduled the summer trip, it had caught me off guard, and before I could even think about it, we had to go.

Lori walked in front of me, her thick dark hair swinging across her back. I was glad she had come with my dad to see me off, but I couldn't even tell her how scared I was. I had only been on a few family trips. Nowhere like Haiti, and never by myself. Even the idea of spending time with Josh couldn't quiet the butterflies in my stomach.

Josh spotted me and gave me a smile. His dark hair and eyes and that chiseled jaw made my heart flutter, forcing me to do battle with my thoughts each time I saw him.

"You okay? You look a little pale."

"Thanks."

"You know what I mean," he said. He put one hand on my shoulder and used the other hand to lift my chin. "Are you okay?"

I took a deep breath. I didn't want to seem like some little girl who needed rescuing. "I'm okay. Just a little nervous about planes. That's all."

He dropped his hand away from my face, and I forced a smile onto it.

"Then I'll pray for God to comfort your heart." Josh bowed his head and prayed. He was always doing that. He wasn't one of those people who said, "I'll pray for you" and then probably went away and forgot about it. He always prayed right then and there. As he finished, though, I really did feel a little calmer.

"Haiti team. Listen up." David Bay, the pastor who was leading the group, jumped up on one of the chairs. He was only a couple inches taller than I, so I understood why he needed the help. "Say your good-byes, grab all of your bags, and let's get in line. We need to get moving."

David jumped off the chair, and everybody began to dismantle the pile of luggage and filter into the roped line at the Delta desk in front of us. Dad walked over to me and squeezed me into a big hug. "So, you ready to go, Butterfly?"

"I guess I don't have a choice." I pulled back. "I'll be okay. Right?"

"It will be great," he said.

"How do you know?"

"I just do. Here, I got something for you." Dad took a small wrapped box from his pocket and handed it to me. I pulled off the pale blue ribbon and paper. I knew he must have gotten it wrapped somewhere, because wrapping was never one of his strong points. I slipped the cover off the box and found a delicate blue butterfly hanging by its wings from a gold chain.

"Dad. It's beautiful." I pulled it from the wrapping, and Dad took it from me and fastened it around my neck. "Thanks."

He squeezed me in another hug. "I'll be praying for you every day."

"I know you will."

"Beka! Come on," Josh called from the end of the line.

"I better go."

"Go. Take care."

Lori came over with my last bag. "Wow!" she said, fingering the butterfly around my neck. "Have fun. I'll miss you."

"I'll miss you too. You can always go hang out with Gretchen while I'm gone."

"Ha-ha. Very funny. I'll wait for you to get back, thank you very much."

"Beka!" Josh's eyes were now wide as he disappeared deeper into the line.

"I gotta go." I gave Lori and my dad each one last hug and hauled my luggage into the line. There was no turning back now.

❦   ❦   ❦

By the time we all climbed onto the plane at 6 a.m. I was too tired to care where I was going anymore. All I wanted to do was go back to sleep. We were scattered all over the plane, and I couldn't even see Josh from where I was sitting. Then a guy who looked a little bit like a Cro-Magnon man with a business suit stared down at me from the aisle.

"So where are you going, little missy?" he asked before he had even stowed his carry-on bag. I tried to remember where my headphones were. Rats. They were in my checked bags.

"Haiti." I turned my attention to my seat belt.

"Haiti? Now that's odd."

I smiled. Maybe if I didn't answer he'd leave me alone. I turned and looked out the window just to make the point.

He wedged himself next to me. "I'm going to Miami myself. Mind if I take off my jacket?"

I waved my hand at him and then instantly wished I

had said I did mind. The smell of cigarettes, liquor, and other odors I didn't want to identify wafted over me. I tried not to crinkle my nose, but I couldn't help it. He stunk.

"Yeah, just flew into town for business. So why Haiti?"

I couldn't believe I was actually going to have to talk to this guy. I looked around to see if anybody on my team was near me. Dana was in the center section one row back, but she seemed engrossed in a conversation with the elderly woman sitting next to her.

I turned to the man while trying to press myself as close to the window as I could get. "I'm going with my church."

"Church. Hummph. Don't have any use for the place myself."

What was I supposed to say? I yanked my backpack out from under the seat and pulled out a book. Maybe that would do the trick.

"You young people. Guess believing won't do much harm." He adjusted himself in his seat and yanked the strap of his seat belt to tighten it. "Me and God aren't exactly on speakin' terms, if you know what I mean."

Who did this guy think he was? I pressed my forehead on the window and watched the airport guys fold up the ramp that had just finished carrying our bags into the belly of the plane.

Fortunately for me, Mr. Cro-Magnon fell asleep as soon as the plane lifted in the air. His mouth drooped open and he snored, but it was better than having to answer all his questions.

I did wonder what might have happened that made him so bitter. Did he lose someone and never get over it? Or maybe he just always did things his own way and was never told anything different. I didn't know anything about how to explain my faith to someone else—I always seemed to just clam up like that. It was another one of those things that I thought I should learn but didn't know where to start. And the thought crossed my mind that I should have been at least nice to the guy.

I watched the clouds in the sky and read a little as we made the trip.

When we descended into the Miami airport, I saw the roads and houses and cars come into view. So many people. I felt so small.

I did say good-bye to Mr. Cro-Magnon as we left the plane, but he seemed groggy from sleeping, and I wasn't sure he really even noticed.

We had to change planes in Miami, so we piled into the waiting area at the gate. Pastor David sent us all off to get some food, and then we had to meet at a new gate for a team meeting. I checked my watch. We had only forty-five minutes before we had to be back. Josh came up next to me.

"Should we go find some food?" he asked.

"Sure." I loved it when he focused on me like that. A few other young people joined us. One skinny guy with glasses seemed about my age. He had introduced himself as Darrin York at one of the team meetings. He seemed shy but nice. Two other girls came over too. One who was a bit younger than I, Caitie Karraker, was bubbly and anything but shy. She kept touching Josh, which bothered me, but it was the tall, pretty brunette named Andi—"it's Andi with an i"—who worried me more. She had to be college age, and before we had even gotten in line to get our lunch, she told us about wanting to go to medical school. Since Josh had been planning on medical school most of his life, they had an instant connection.

We took our trays, and after pulling two tables together, I made a maneuver to sit next to Josh. I managed to do it, but because of the table legs we were still at separate tables. And Andi plopped herself down right across from him, which left me talking with Darrin and Caitie. They were nice, but I couldn't get my mind off of Andi and Josh, leaning close together and sharing their passion for medicine as they ate their lunch.

"So how long have you been going to Harvest Fellowship?" Caitie asked me.

"Oh. Five years, I guess. Something like that," I said. I stirred my straw in my soda and watched Andi pat Josh's forearm.

"We came last year. What about you, Darrin?" she asked.

"Two years and three months," he said, pushing his glasses back up on his nose. "Aren't you the girl, well, you're the one who . . . that was your mom who died last year, wasn't it?"

I tore my eyes away from Andi and Josh and looked back at Darrin and Caitie. Caitie had gone quiet, and both of them were looking at me.

"Yep. That would be me." I nibbled on a cold French fry.

"What happened?" Caitie tucked her brown hair behind her ear.

"It was a car accident, right?" Darrin said.

"She was coming home from seeing a patient at the hospital and had an accident on the ice. It happened a year ago last March." I said it like a robot. I didn't feel like baring my soul to two almost-strangers in an airport. Caitie and Darrin just stared at me. Andi and Josh had stopped talking and were staring at me too. I shifted in my seat. Now I needed rescuing.

"We better get back for that meeting," Josh said. He stood up and began to gather the trash at the table. Everyone else followed his lead, and we walked back to the new gate. I walked behind everybody else feeling uncomfortable. It was always like that when my mom came up. People either didn't know what to say or they gushed all over me about how sorry they were. But I always left feeling odd and out of place.

Josh dropped back to walk with me.

"Thanks," I said.

"No problem," he said. "I'm glad you're here, Beka. Really."

I let his words sink into me. It was just something new. An adventure. Right? So what that I had no idea what I was getting into. I was with Josh. And that was all that mattered at the moment.

The descent

into Port-au-Prince, Haiti, was very different from the descent into Miami. I had snagged another window seat, and I watched as we landed at an airport that looked like nothing more than a dilapidated strip mall. They rolled a stairway out to the plane, and stepping outside was like stepping into hot soup. We went straight from the plane to our pile of luggage and through customs. We were carrying over-the-counter medicines to distribute, and Pastor Dave got hung up trying to explain it to the customs officers in Creole.

When they finally let us through, we went out onto the street and were piled into three pickup trucks that had been converted into taxis. A multicolored cabin with benches had been mounted onto the back of each truck, and we crammed ourselves into two of them, and our luggage went into the third. I got a seat on the end of the bench so I wasn't stuck underneath the little cabin. I watched the city bounce by as we made our way down the streets. It wasn't at all what I expected.

Even though I knew it wouldn't be like an American city, it was a shock to see regular, although mostly old, cars driving down the street, along with donkeys, pigs, and chickens everywhere. I lost count of how many animals I saw walking along the shoulder and darting in and out of traffic. The landscape was lush and green with palm trees and thick vegetation, but most of the buildings were nothing more than cinder block and tin. Many Haitians walked alongside the roads, the women wearing long skirts, just like the one I was wearing. We were told that all the women in our group had to wear long skirts in public, so before the trip I bought several at a thrift store. They were a pretty bad fashion statement, but I was almost glad for the thin fabric because it was so hot.

The truck taxis drove us to a plain two-story house with a flat roof and geometric grates covering the doorway and windows. Standing at the gate to greet us was Se Tata, our host for the ten-day trip, who was wearing a bright blue suit. She hugged each of us as we crawled out of the taxis. She took us up to the second floor, where we were split into four different bedrooms. Se Tata spoke English, sort of, and she showed us around the house. She had two teenage girls who seemed to help with the housework, but they just nodded shyly at us as we passed by the small kitchen.

I stared at the little bathroom we all had to share. Not only was it small, but the water for the shower apparently just dripped over you from a container on the roof. Oh, and the toilet didn't flush. One of the Haitian girls showed us all how to pour the water into the toilet and use a plunger to force it down the pipes. We were going to have to haul water up to the roof every other day to keep everything working.

I flopped onto one of the cots in my room that I was sharing with Caitie, Andi with an i, and Dana. I wouldn't get any kind of privacy on this trip.

"You guys want to go up on the roof?" Dana asked. She had been to Haiti twice before, so before we even left I made a plan to stick near her. She hung out with the youth pretty often, so I at least knew her a little bit. Dana always seemed to know what she was doing.

"Sure," Caitie said, closing her suitcase. Caitie and Andi followed her out onto a second-story patio, and Dana climbed up a white ladder. We followed her up onto the flat roof, and I walked over to the edge. Right across the street from us was a walled lot that was a small dump on one half with a small cinder block and stone house on the other. The roof was held on with cinder blocks and stones scattered across the top, and I could see a family of pigs curled up near the edge of the pile of garbage.

Down the hill and up the side of the mountain near us were more of the same types of houses, low and plain with flat roofs held together with different bits of material.

Dana appeared next to me and stared off into the city. "What do you think?" she asked.

"It's so poor." I knew it was obvious, but it's all I could think about. Downstairs I had been moaning about the bathroom and the lack of privacy, and here were all these people who lived like this day in and day out. Most of the houses weren't even as nice as Se Tata's.

"See that little girl?" Dana pointed over to the garbage pile where a little black girl, no more than five, was digging through the garbage.

"What's she doing?" I watched her as she rifled through the trash in her bare feet.

"Looking for food, or for something that her parents could sell. Even when they're little, the kids have to work. Some do what she's doing; others are hired out by their families as servants for richer families. They make about twenty-five cents a day."

"Twenty-five cents? A day?" I watched the girl find something that she carefully placed in a cloth bag slung across her skinny shoulders. I just stood there watching the scene before me, wondering how it could even be real. Such a tiny girl. Such filth. It seemed so unfair.

After a while Dana said, "We do some good things while we're down here. But truthfully, I often think they're better off than most Americans."

"Seriously?"

"You'll see." She smiled and went back to the ladder. I sat down and folded my legs underneath me and stared out into the city. It was so different to be there when just yesterday I was packing at home. My cushy, air-conditioned life back home.

I stayed on the roof until I heard somebody yell that it was dinnertime. As I was climbing down the ladder, I realized that not once had I wished that Josh would come and join me. Interesting.

*   *   *

We all gathered around an enormous table where bowls were filled with all sorts of different kinds of foods. Se Tata pointed to each one as she tried to explain what they were. Even though I wasn't too excited about trying a lot of the foods, I took a little of each and plopped them onto my plate. While I picked at the food I watched Andi flirt with Josh near the end of the table.

Why did she have to be here? It made me think about all the girls he would meet at Seattle Pacific. Even though Josh wanted to write to me, it didn't seem likely that it would ever be anything more than friendship. I could get to know him all I wanted, but he would still be three thousand miles away.

And then there was Mark.

I felt a smile creep across my face as I thought about the cute blond guy from back home who had promised to win back my heart.

Even though I was pretty sure he had never lost it to begin with.

The problem was my father, who was very unhappy that I had snuck off with Mark before—even though we didn't really do anything wrong. Dad had said no to actually dating, but it hadn't stopped Mark from making efforts.

My summer could be summed up in two words— guitar and camera. I was taking three guitar lessons a week and working at Lori's mom's photography studio. Mark came by the studio regularly to say hi. We didn't really get to see each other alone, but boy, did he make my heart flutter with his crooked smile and dimple.

Mark told me that he didn't want to be just friends, and even though Josh was sweet, and definitely more spiritual, there was something about Mark that had latched on inside of me. Too bad Mark wasn't here. Then again, it would be weird and definitely confusing to have them both in the same place at the same time.

After dinner was cleaned up, Pastor Dave had us all cram into a small common area for another team meeting. We were divided into three teams. One team would run the medical clinic, one team would run a vacation Bible school, and the last one would be working on repairing the school. Pastor Dave read off the lists. My name was on the Bible school list, while Josh and Andi were on the medical team.

What was I doing here? The whole reason I came was to spend time with Josh, and now I would barely see him. We broke up into our smaller teams to begin making plans. Dana took charge of our group, which included Darrin and Caitie.

Dana had brought supplies for the crafts that we would do with the kids each day, so at least that part was finished. But then Dana said that we could have hundreds of kids show up for the Bible school. Hundreds? I didn't even like babysitting, and I was going to help run a Bible school with hundreds of kids who, by the way, didn't speak English?

I wanted to go home.

I was put in charge of music. When Dana found out I played the guitar, she said, "Okay then, you and Kyle can do the music."

"But I just started playing. I don't think I can do it."

Dana waved her hand at me. "You'll do fine. Besides, that's why I put you with Kyle."

"But I don't have my guitar with me. How am I supposed to—"

"Beka, it will be fine. You can use Pastor Dave's."

There was no arguing with Dana. And so Kyle and I spent almost the entire weekend on the roof working on the music. Or, to be honest, Kyle spent the whole weekend teaching me to play the songs we were going to teach the kids.

I felt so stupid because I really didn't go to church till I was ten, so I never learned all the little Bible songs and stories that they were talking about. Kyle was patient with me. He was in college, but he looked like a beach bum. He was tall and had a ratty beard, and he always wore grubby T-shirts and pants that looked like they might unravel at any minute. But he was fun and a very good teacher. When Monday came, I knew I could at least keep up on the guitar and with the singing, even if I didn't do anything else.

*   *   *

Monday morning I stumbled out into the hallway and tripped over a turkey wandering around in the upstairs hallway. I had thought the strange gobbling sounds I heard were just part of a dream, but there really was a turkey strutting down to one of the other bedrooms. I rubbed my eyes, trying to decide why a turkey was in the house, when one of the young girls that worked for Se Tata came running up the stairs and pounced on the big bird, scolding it in Creole. She smiled and nodded at me before running back down the stairs with the turkey.

I shook my head and shuffled to the bathroom. What a way to wake up.

We walked to the church as one large group, wandering in and out of the dirt and gravel streets of Port-au-Prince. People sat on the stoops of the storefronts and homes, staring at us. Kids started gathering around us, holding out their hands and speaking to us in Creole. A little girl in a tattered blue dress slipped her hand inside of mine as I walked. She looked up at me with a shy smile. A block later a little boy grabbed my other hand and swung it back and forth. When I looked around at the group, every free hand of our team had been claimed. The kids that hadn't found a hand ran alongside of us, chattering away. Some children were trying to help Kyle carry the two guitars, and Josh was carrying one little boy and had the hand of another one. Caitie had two little girls with her.

It was so surreal.

I began to notice a long line of Haitians standing and sitting along the side of the road. People from little kids to old men and women were waiting for something, but it wasn't until we turned into the church gate that I realized they were in line for the medical clinic. So many people were waiting that I didn't think there was any way they could all be seen. Later, Pastor Dave told us that if they didn't get in today they would probably stay in line till the next morning.

I thought of my mom, who had been a pediatrician. How she would have loved to have been here with me. Tears sprang into my eyes when we rounded the corner and I saw the hundreds of children gathered in the courtyard. When they saw us, they let out a yell as if we were some traveling rock band and they were our fans.

I gasped as they barreled toward us.

They surrounded our small group with huge smiles, rambling on in Creole. All my jitters about playing in front of a crowd of people melted away. These kids wouldn't care how good or bad I was. They just wanted us here.

*　　*　　*

The day was a whirlwind. The girl who had held my hand never left my side. The songs were a hit, and the craft was chaotic, but you would have thought we were giving the kids gold coins instead of twine and beads. When we had finished the formal part of the Bible school lessons, the guys played games in the courtyard with them, carrying the kids on their backs and swinging them around in circles. Every once in a while I checked the line at the medical clinic as the people moved through the lines. Many of the men and women were gaunt, and some could barely seem to stand up.

I wandered over and went to the back door of the medical clinic where Serg and Gary, two of the men from our team, were manning a table filled with over-the-counter drugs. They gave me a wave as I ducked into a smaller room to the left of the main room of the building. From there I could see into the main examining room where four different stations were set up. Josh was there in the middle of it all.

I watched him take temperatures and pulses and talk to each of the Haitians through a young translator. He really didn't do anything spectacular, but seeing him in that place, helping people, reassuring mothers, I got a glimpse of everything I knew he would become.

I snuck back out before he even saw me, and as

soon as I stepped into the courtyard, several of the kids brought me a guitar and pushed it into my hands, silently asking me to play for them. At first I sat down on the ground, but then I had to go find a chair as more and more kids crushed in on top of me. The group followed me over to the old benches to the right of the courtyard, and I put the guitar strap over my shoulder. I played everything I knew for them, which wasn't a whole lot, but they seemed to love it. Kyle came over and joined me, and the crowd of kids grew larger and larger. We made up silly songs, and even though the kids didn't understand the words, they laughed at the funny faces we made. My new little friend had squeezed in beside me on the bench, her hands folded on her lap as she listened and smiled at me.

It was a great day, and that night around our dinner table I found out why I had met a turkey in the hallway that morning: because now it was sitting in the center of the table, roasted a golden brown.

The three days that followed were just about the same. We didn't do much more than play with the kids after the Bible school was over for the day, but they were so happy about it. I found out that the little girl who was following me around was named Maria. She stuck close to me each day and took charge of my guitar case, shaking her finger and scolding anyone who came near it. What amazed me was that these kids had so much joy even though they had so little. It was the opposite in America—so many people unhappy, even though they had so much.

And it was the same with the older people. We visited

one woman's home that stood on a small hill right off of a river of what looked like sewage. The smell was powerful, yet the whole family smiled as they showed us their simple, tiny home. The mother beamed with pride when she pointed to a small painting hanging on the wall. They didn't have much "stuff," but they seemed to know a lot more about joy than I ever did. They were just so content.

My own suffering seemed so small in that place.

I fell into bed exhausted each night but usually lay awake thinking about my mom and how much I wanted to talk with her. She was the one person I wanted to share this with. To tell her what was happening around me. And in me.

The world just seemed bigger than I had imagined, and I felt smaller. Not insignificant, just smaller. I didn't know how to describe it to anyone, really. I spent hours up on Se Tata's roof looking out over this city.

After we finished up the Bible school and the clinic, they took us out to the beach for a day trip. I was amazed at this beautiful beach in the countryside in such a poor country. We ate stalks of raw sugarcane and played a game of volleyball with a makeshift net. I caught Josh smiling at me more than once, and even though we didn't get much time to talk, it no longer seemed to matter.

*   *   *

The hardest day was when we went and visited an orphanage where the children were dying of AIDS and other diseases. Beautiful little children and babies just wasting away in white metal cribs. And there were so many of them. Three levels of open rooms, and each had row after row of little children, completely alone in their cribs, staring through the bars without even the strength to sit up. It felt like someone was squeezing my heart inside of my chest. We wandered around the different wards, talking to the kids, holding them. Pastor Dave told us that with so many children and so few workers, the kids never really got held, and so that was our mission that day—to hold them and love on them. I prayed for each little baby I picked up, but it somehow seemed like such a little effort for so great a need. I fought back the tears more than once. If I cared about them, how much more did God care about them? And yet they were still going to die.

There was so much about God that I just didn't understand.

I certainly couldn't do anything to help them. I picked up one little girl who weighed almost nothing and rocked her, singing a made-up lullaby to her.

Josh walked up beside me with a tiny little baby in his arms.

"I wish there was something I could do to help them," I said.

"Yeah. There's so many of them." Josh rubbed his fingers along the baby's face and then looked over at me.

"You glad you came?"

I nodded. "It's a lot harder than I thought it would be. But a lot better too." I shifted the little girl into my other arm. "I guess you're leaving as soon as we get back."

"We land on Monday, and I leave Tuesday." He paused. "I'm sorry we didn't get to spend much time together. I was hoping . . . well . . ."

"It's okay. Kyle's been teaching me more stuff on the guitar. I wrote my first song."

Josh grinned. "Really? Can I hear it?"

"Absolutely not. It's a silly song that we did for the kids, but it was really cool. I kind of know what I need to do now to write a real song."

"That's great. Promise me you'll let me hear your first real song."

"We'll see. You're going to be pretty far away."

"I know. Look, I know we promised to write, but I don't want you to feel like you can't . . ." Josh took a deep breath. "I don't want you to feel any obligation toward me."

I let his words sink in. No obligations.

I moved toward the crib and laid the little girl back down, adjusting her blankets before I turned back to Josh. I could get lost in those eyes.

"No obligation, huh?"

"What I mean is . . . I can't promise you anything."

"I'm not asking you to," I said.

"I know you're not." Josh dropped his head back and closed his eyes for a moment. He opened them back up. "Let's take a walk, okay?"

I followed him over to one of the cribs, where he laid his baby back down. He turned and used his head to gesture toward the door. I followed him down the stairs out into a small cement courtyard with a dry, crumbling fountain right in the center. We sat in the only spot where the concrete still formed a small ledge.

"We're not going to get a chance to talk again, and since I've already missed a couple of days of school, I'm going to be pretty busy."

"I figured." I felt all nervous and upset. I would have thought he was breaking up with me if we had been going out.

"You just weren't a part of things. When I got into Seattle Pacific we barely knew each other, and now I don't know what to do. There's nothing I can do, of course."

"What?"

Josh turned toward me. "The timing is just bad. I can't ask you to commit to me when I can't be here for you. But I want to. I want to tell you that I don't want you to see anybody else. Ask you to wait for me. But I can't do that to you."

"I didn't know . . . I mean, I wasn't really sure if you felt . . ." I stuttered trying to get the words to come out.

Josh cocked his head at me and smiled. "Beka, you're the sweetest girl I've ever known." His smile faded. "I'm going to miss you."

"Me too." I looked down at my lap, unsure what to say next. I really liked Josh. I felt safe and secure with him. He was tall, with deep brown eyes and dark hair, but he was so much more than nice to look at. He had goals, and I had no doubt that he would be a great doctor one day. He cared about people. On the inside, he seemed a lot older than eighteen.

But Mark was so different. Josh made my heart feel safe and unrushed, but Mark said things to me that sent shivers through my soul. I felt so confused. How could my heart be going in two different directions at one time?

And what did God think of it all?

That was the million-dollar question.

I hadn't been a real Christian for very long, and it was still so confusing to me to know how to follow God. How are you supposed to know what He is saying to you? How can you follow somebody if you don't know where they're going? Josh moving to Seattle seemed like the answer, but as we sat there, I didn't feel sure about that at all. I couldn't bear the thought of him falling for someone out in Seattle.

I looked back over to where Josh had leaned up against the crumbling fountain.

"So what do we do now?"

"Keep in touch. Maybe you can go to Seattle Pacific when you graduate." He pushed my shoulder playfully when he said it, but his eyes were serious.

College. Another dilemma I didn't have the energy to think about. I had to write applications in the next couple of months, and I didn't even know where I wanted to go. I couldn't imagine going across the country though. Leave my family?

Then again, my family would already be different when I got home. We had taken my older brother, Paul, to college just before I left for Haiti, so he wouldn't be there. It would just be me, my two little sisters, Lucy and Anna, and my dad. Lucy would be going to Bragg County High as a freshman this year.

So many changes. I didn't know what to think about it all.

I looked over at Josh. There just didn't seem to be anything else to say. We stood up, and Josh took my hand as we walked back up to the third floor of the orphanage.

So how was it?" Dad asked after I had said my good-byes to the team and we were finally on the road. It was late, and I was wiped out, but I filled him in on the main parts of the trip.

Then I closed my eyes. "It was really good. I'm glad I went." I lifted the handle on the side of the seat and let the seat drop back. I was so tired. "Have you heard from Paul?"

"Yes. His classes started last week. Apparently he has to take a seventeen-credit load every semester to take all the classes he'll need to get into medical school."

"Is that a lot?"

"Well, it's just a little on the high side, but his classes are bound to be tough."

"And Anna and Lucy?"

"Lucy's been at the gym every day, and we might as well rent Anna a stall next to Wind Dancer."

That meant that Anna was out at Gabby's farm every day. Gabby was the single woman who had wormed her way into my family through her horse farm and her offer to board my sister's new horse. Dad had promised me they weren't "involved," but I knew that she was interested in more than friendship. If Dad ever decided to marry her, I might have to apply to Seattle Pacific just to get away from her.

*   *   *

"So tell me every detail," Lori said after she belly-flopped onto my bed. Megan, her mom, had dropped her off so that she could spend the night.

I told Lori all about the trip and the orphanage. I didn't tell her about Josh though. That deserved its own conversation.

"What about you?" I asked. "I guess Brian's gone already."

"Yeah, he left on Thursday. It's going to be so weird not seeing him every day."

"How did you leave things?"

"Well, he'll be coming home sometimes, but we're not going to be able to see each other much." Lori rolled over and looked up at the ceiling. "But we're not going to see anybody else. That's for sure."

"So you're gonna do the long-distance thing?"

"We have to. I couldn't imagine being with anyone else."

"Lori, you only met him eight months ago."

"And I knew then. We had this kind of instant connection." Lori rolled back over and eyed me. "What's wrong?"

"Nothing, why?" I pulled my knees up to my chest and rested my chin on top.

"You're being cynical. So something's bothering you."

I climbed off the bed and paced to my desk and then to my dresser and back to the bed. By that time Lori was sitting up, patiently waiting for my answer.

"Why can't things make sense for me?"

"Are you talking about Josh?" she asked.

"And Mark."

Lori crinkled her nose at Mark's name.

"I know how you feel about him, but you don't really know him."

"I know he's gotten you grounded three times already."

"I got myself grounded. It was my fault, not his."

"Really? Like you would have snuck off with him on your own. Tell me he didn't bat his blue eyes at you, comb his fingers through his blond hair, and ask you to come with him."

"He asked, yes, but I knew better than to do it without asking. You can't blame him."

"Beka." Lori sighed. "I hate talking about Mark, because we always end up arguing."

I sat back down on the bed.

"What about Josh?" Lori asked.

"He's probably packing right now. He leaves in the morning. And he doesn't want me to feel obligated."

"What does that mean?"

"It means we're friends. He says he's going to write me, but who knows? I'm sure there are plenty of pretty college girls who'll keep him busy."

"I'm sorry."

"I'm going to see Mark every day. I probably won't see Josh again till Christmas."

"And you like them both. So what are you going to do?"

As I thought about the answer to that question, which of course I had only thought about a hundred times, my phone rang. "Hello?" I answered.

"Can you come outside?"

"Mark? Where are you?"

"Standing underneath your window. I heard you were back."

I walked over to my window and looked out. Lori came to the window too. Mark was standing on the lawn with a cell phone to his ear. When he spotted us he waved.

"Please? Just for a minute?" he said.

"Give me three minutes," I said. I hung up the phone, and Lori and I moved away from the window.

"What does he want?" Lori asked.

"I don't know. I'm going down," I said. Lori flashed me a look. "It's just for a minute. It's fine." I slipped my shoes back on and left without looking at Lori. I knew she wasn't happy.

I managed to slip down the stairs and out the front door without being seen. Mark was waiting right where I had seen him from the window. I walked toward him, my heart pounding in my chest. I hadn't seen him in weeks. He looked wonderful. I stopped near him, but when I stopped, he instantly closed the gap and wrapped his arms around me and squeezed.

"I missed you," he said. He pulled away enough to look at me. He stared into my eyes just long enough to make me fidget; then he leaned in and kissed me. A soft, gentle kiss. I didn't try to stop him.

"Perfect," he said.

All the excuses and reasons I shouldn't be standing there stampeded through my head. All the questions about what we were to each other swirled around. I didn't even want to talk. I just wanted to stand like that with his arms around me forever.

But I couldn't.

"I better go back inside," I said.

Mark groaned. "Already?" He pulled me closer.

I smiled. I liked that he didn't want to go. "School starts next week. We'll see each other every day."

"You promise?"

I smiled again. "Yeah. I promise."

"What about your dad? Will he reconsider letting us be official? So I can take you out on a real date?"

I took in a deep breath. "I don't know. I'll try to talk to him." Even as I said the words the thought of actually bringing up the topic with Dad made my stomach flip over.

"I guess that'll have to do," he said.

"You need to let me go."

"I can't."

"Mark."

"Okay, okay." He kissed me again before he unwrapped his arms from me. "I'll see you soon. And I do want to hear about Haiti."

We said good-bye, and I slipped back up to my room, unable to remove the grin from my face. Lori looked up from the book she was reading when I got back in. She shook her head softly.

"Beka. I can't believe you."

"Oh, Lori. Just be happy for me. He's just so amazing."

Lori lifted an eyebrow at me. "Go down and tell your dad, and then I'll be happy for you."

I pushed out my bottom lip and folded my arms. "Come on. I just have to give Dad some time."

Lori huffed and then smiled. "So what did he say?"

Now don't go crazy with this." Dad held out his credit card, but when I reached to take it he wouldn't let it go.

"I promise, we'll behave. But there's three of us, and clothes are expensive."

"I know." He let go of the credit card, and I slipped it into my bag.

"Okay, girls. Time to shop," I said.

Dad groaned. Lucy and Anna went out the door. "I'll bring back every receipt."

He lifted half his mouth with a sigh. "That's what I'm afraid of."

We drove to the mall so that I could make sure Anna

and Lucy had everything they needed for school. I had already gotten most of my own things, and all I had left to get were some shoes. Even though shopping wasn't my favorite thing to do, I found myself looking forward to going back to school. I was finally a senior, I had a job as the editor of our school newspaper, *The Bragg About,* and Mark liked me. What more could I ask for? The only black cloud on the horizon was Gretchen and Mai. Gretchen spent her entire summer vacation in detention for setting up the attack on me, and I knew Mai must have been in on it too, even though she didn't get in trouble. They were always together, so she must have known what Gretchen was planning. I didn't want to face them, but I couldn't live in fear of them either.

As soon as we got to the mall, Anna and Lucy wanted to go in two different directions, so I let Lucy head to her favorite store while I took Anna to a couple of the kids' stores. She was only nine, but she was pretty serious about what she wanted to wear.

"I like the blue shirt, but the fabric for these pants is gross," she said.

"Well, get these instead. It'll still match, and these are much softer." I held out a pair of cords to her.

"Perfect." She smiled. "I'm glad you're taking me school shopping and not Dad. He's so yesterday."

I laughed. "He tries hard."

"I know. But fourth grade is a big deal. I need to be the most popular girl."

"No, you don't, Anna. You just need to be you."

Anna rolled her eyes. "Beka, you know very well that popularity is important."

"Important to who?" I dumped her clothes on the counter to pay for them.

"Me."

"So what makes you popular in the fourth grade anyway?"

"Rebekah?"

I turned around to see Gretchen's mother, Mrs. Stanley, standing behind me. She was holding Gretchen's little sister, Stacy, by the hand. Stacy was in the same grade as Anna, and they said hello to each other. Just behind her mother, Gretchen stood with her arms crossed. She wasn't wearing any makeup, and her hair looked like she had just pulled a brush through it. She wore a rumpled T-shirt and some blue athletic pants, like what you might wear when you're hanging around the house. There was a long, awkward pause as I tried to get a handle on seeing a very different Gretchen. She stared at the floor as her mother started talking.

"Rebekah, I just wanted to tell you, to let you know how sorry I am . . ." She put her hand to her mouth like she were catching a sob. "I can't believe what Gretchy did. I mean, I did not raise my girl to be a criminal, I assure you, but we are so sorry for what happened to you. I mean, what happened to you is horrible, but she's ruined her own life too. She may not even be able to get into college now . . ." Her hand flew to her mouth again as she choked on a sob.

I felt Anna slip her hand into mine, and I slid a look at Gretchen. She hadn't moved.

When she composed herself, Mrs. Stanley continued, "It was the most dreadful thing, and to think your own flesh and blood could be that cold-blooded. Well, there's still hope for my Stacy." She pulled Stacy's hand up to her chest. "I wasn't even going to send Gretchen back to that school, but, well, she's not to bother you at all, I assure you. I'm so sorry. Really and truly." Mrs. Stanley stood and looked at me for a minute, then nodded and pulled Stacy along beside her toward the front door of the store. Gretchen turned and followed like a robot.

"Is that the horrible girl who got you hurt?" Anna asked.

I nodded and watched them leave, still unable to think of anything to say. I actually felt sorry for Gretchen.

Anna and I bought her clothes and then went to meet Lucy in the food court for lunch. Anna and Lucy were talking about school when I noticed Mark walking across the far side of the food court. He was carrying a black plastic bag and sipping a soda.

Boy, was he cute. I knew he couldn't see me, so I just watched him.

"What do you think, Beka?"

"Huh?" I tore my eyes away from Mark and looked at Lucy.

"What's your problem?" Lucy asked.

"Nothing. I just didn't hear you." I glanced up to find Mark, who was now over by the sunglass kiosk, and then looked back at Lucy. "So. What?"

"We were thinking that we could go looking for shoes after you go pay for the stuff they're holding for me at Aeropostale."

"Shoes, sure," I said. Mark moved away from the kiosk and looked around the food court as if he were trying to find someone. I wondered who he could be meeting. I stared at him, willing him to see me.

And he did. Our eyes locked, and a smile spread across his face. We stayed that way for a minute, but he made no move to come over to our table. Smart guy. I didn't need Anna and Lucy getting my dad all worked up about running into a friend at the mall. Right?

Mark tossed his bag onto one of the tables near him and sat down, never taking his eyes off me. I knew exactly what to do.

"Hey, Lucy. Why don't you guys go look for shoes, I'll go buy your stuff, and then we'll meet a little later? I need to look for a few things."

Lucy shrugged. "Whatever. I'm done anyway. But don't take anything out of my pile. You have to buy it all."

"Fine, fine," I said.

After just a few minutes, Anna and Lucy left in one direction, and I made a beeline for Mark. I tried not to seem too eager, but I knew I was grinning.

"Hey, Beautiful," he said as I pulled out a chair across from him. I sat down and leaned back casually.

"Hey, yourself," I said. "What is it? Shoes?"

"Yep, even guys need to go shopping now and then."

"Is that all you're getting?"

"I want to kiss you."

"What?"

"You heard me."

"It's not happening here. This place is crawling with people who know my dad. He's got eyes everywhere. If it's not somebody from church, it's somebody from the bank."

Mark grimaced.

"Besides. We talked about this. We're going to cool it on the physical part, right? We can't go out."

"That's not fair. You let me kiss you the other night."

I closed my eyes and remembered. "Well, I shouldn't have. And you promised not to push."

"Yeah, yeah, yeah. I know."

"Besides. Say my dad tells me that we can go out."

"Did you talk to him?"

"No. Hypothetically. What if he said we can date?"

"Then we'd go out." He drew his eyebrows together. "What are you getting at?"

"I don't know. Never mind. Look, I have to go buy Lucy's school clothes."

"I'll go with you." Mark stood up and grabbed his bag and soda and walked with me to Aeropostale. My chest felt tight and uncomfortable. I wished God would just tell me what I was supposed to do. It was so confusing trying to figure it out on my own. Mark walked close to me and carried half my bags. I loved having Mark around, and he always made me feel so special, but I was uncomfortable with the physical stuff. I liked it when he kissed me and held me the other night. I really did. But I couldn't help but wonder what would happen if the relationship were official. How much would he expect?

And how far was too far?

It was the only thing about Mark that scared me. And in a weird way, my dad saying no to dating actually helped. I needed more time to figure out where I stood on the whole purity issue. If it were as simple as sex or no sex, it would be easier. But it was way more complicated than that. I had already figured that out first-hand with Mark. Plus, I knew Mark was very experienced in that department.

I paid for Lucy's enormous pile of clothes—knowing Dad was going to have a heart attack when he saw the receipt, but I wasn't going to fight Lucy's battle.

"How much time do you have?" Mark asked.

"Maybe twenty minutes." I figured that would give me enough time to buy some shoes before meeting Lucy and Anna.

Mark led me toward the far end of the mall where there was an alcove of benches and trees, kind of like a small indoor garden. I found it strange to be inside a mall with so much . . . stuff. After Haiti it all seemed so unnecessary. He sat down on a bench and turned to face me.

He smiled. "I'm sorry I said that."

"What?"

"About kissing you, and our kiss the other night. I did promise to back off in that area." He picked my hand up off my leg and rubbed it with his thumb. "I'll try. Really. It's just that when you're near me I want to hold you and kiss you. I can't help it."

"Well, I'm not exactly an innocent bystander," I said. And I definitely wasn't. Especially since I liked it when he kissed me. But would it be enough for him? I pushed the questions out of my head. It made me tired to never get any answers. I felt like a hamster spinning on a wheel.

When it was time to say good-bye, Mark leaned over and gave me a lingering kiss on the cheek, then winked at me before he left. Leave it to Mark. I ran off to get my shoes and find Lucy and Anna, my heart still thumping in my chest, but my mind already deciding which shoe store to hit first.

*   *   *

"That doesn't sound at all like Gretchen," Lori said when I filled her in on my run-in with the Stanleys at the mall. "That's so weird."

"I know. I can't believe her mom said all those things. Right in front of her." I picked at the fringe on my carpet, pulling it up, then smoothing it down.

"I can't believe she's going to be back in school," Lori said. "I don't know what I'd do if I were in your place. After what she did?"

"I don't think I'm going to have to worry about Gretchen anymore."

"What do you mean?"

"She just seemed different. More like a wounded puppy than a pit bull ready to attack."

"I hope you're right."

"You know I'm supposed to forgive her."

"And?"

"I don't know. I prefer not to think about it. Just move on. Forget about it. You know?"

"Yeah, I know."

*   *   *

Long after Lori hung up, I thought about Gretchen. I couldn't conjure up any emotions.

Not anger, not fear. I felt nothing. What did it look like to forgive someone anyway? Did it mean I had to like her? Trust her? I didn't really want to do either. If I wasn't mad about it anymore, did that mean I had already forgiven her? The questions swirled around and around until I was too tired to think. I didn't even want to look in my Bible. I was sure that would just bring up even more questions.

And what I needed was answers.

It was the beginning of the end. Finally. It would be my last year at Bragg County High School. I could hardly believe it. And even though I didn't know where I was headed when I finally did get to graduate, it still felt good to be a senior.

And it didn't hurt that Mark was waiting for me at the door.

Lucy was with me, with the nerves typical of every freshman. She seemed younger here than she seemed at home. Mark smiled as we approached.

"Hey there," he said. I was glad he didn't call me "Beautiful" in front of Lucy. Mark was always quick to weigh a situation.

"Good morning. You've met my sister Lucy. She's a frosh."

"Yeah, we met briefly." Mark smiled at her, and Lucy smiled shyly.

"Can I walk you two to class?" Mark asked.

"Sure. So how ya doing?" I asked. We walked toward the freshman wing first, where Lucy would have homeroom.

"I'm great. I saw your name on Thompson's theory list. We're actually going to have a class together."

"And you have access to this list how?"

"I'm his senior aide. So I got a peek at the class lists."

"Why would you be taking music theory?"

"I'm not, but it's my free period, so I'll be helping him out." Mark grinned at me.

"Here you go, Luce. It's that room." I pointed across the hall, and Lucy let out a squeal.

"Aaaaammmyyy!" Lucy ran over and hugged her friend as if they hadn't seen each other in years.

"All right, I'm going," I said.

Lucy waved at me but seemed to be fine as she talked with Amy and her other friends. They all clung to each other as if they were afraid they might be separated. I turned to Mark, and he moved up close to me. We walked down the hallway, and as soon as we turned the corner he slipped his hand in mine.

It felt good. He walked with me to my locker and then to my homeroom before he ran off to his class. What a way to start the new year.

*   *   *

Lori and I had the same lunch period and three classes together, so everything was shaping up pretty well. When we sat down to lunch, Mark walked over with his tray.

"Mind if I sit with you ladies?"

"Go for it," I said.

Lori smiled politely but did not look happy. I promised myself I'd talk to her about it later. I couldn't believe Mark was really there.

"So how's your morning?" he asked.

I glanced at Lori, then smiled at Mark. "Good so far. Lori and I have more classes together this year, so that's cool."

"I saw your friend Gretchen this morning," he said.

"Funny." I smirked at him.

"She looks rough."

"I saw her before first. Just in the hallway though. We don't have any classes together. They might have done that on purpose," I said.

"What about journalism? There's only one class of that," Lori asked.

"I don't know. I guess she could be in there." The thought settled in my stomach. It would be fine, right?

"I guess a summer of detention took a piece out of her. Maybe that's a good thing," Lori said.

"Maybe." I poked at the salad on my tray. "But it seems like more than that. Something's really wrong."

"Of course there is," Mark said. "She set you up to be attacked. You got stabbed. You could have gotten raped. She shouldn't even be here this year."

"I agree. But she is here. I just hope she learned her

lesson and leaves us alone." Lori stood up. "We better go."

Mark stood up and walked to the trash cans with us. He smiled at me. "Well, we can walk to theory together. Lori, what do you have?"

"I've got French One. It's in the freshman quad," she answered, but her body language made it clear she didn't want him there, invading our lunchtime. We walked through the common area and toward the freshman area.

"So Brian tells me you're the best thing that ever happened to him," Mark said.

Lori blushed but said nothing.

Mark turned and looked at me, brushing my hand with his.

"Hey, that's Lucy. What's Mai doing here?" Lori pointed toward the right side of the hallway.

I looked and saw Lucy deep in conversation with Mai, Gretchen's best friend. What *was* she doing there? I moved away from Mark and Lori and went up to Lucy.

"So how is it?" I asked her. Mai leveled her gaze at me, and Lucy smiled.

"Not bad. Once I get used to where everything is. Mai says she knows you."

"Mai, you don't have any classes this way. What's up?" I didn't ask in a friendly way, and she noticed.

"Fifty-Fifty Mentors. I help a whole group of freshmen get used to the school. And I just happened to get your sister here." Mai smiled, but I narrowed my eyes at her.

"Leave Lucy alone," I said.

"Beka!" Lucy said.

"She's Gretchen's friend, Lucy. You should just stay away from her." I took Lucy's arm to leave with her, but she pulled it away.

"She doesn't hang out with Gretchen anymore. And she didn't have anything to do with what happened to you."

"And you believe her?"

Lucy paused and looked between Mai and me. "Yes. She said Gretchen's gone nuts, and she doesn't want anything to do with her anymore."

I shook my head. "You can't trust her. Don't be so gullible."

Lucy's eyebrows drew together, and she hiked her backpack up on her shoulder. "I don't need your help, Beka. Let me make my own friends."

"Not with her you can't."

Lucy turned and walked away, leaving Mai standing with me and smiling. She tucked her silky black hair behind her ear and leaned toward me. "Don't worry, Beka. I'll take real good care of her."

It sounded like a threat.

I walked back over to Lori and Mark and told them what was going on, but the bell rang, and we had to run. I spent my first class with Mark worrying about Lucy. And Mai. I knew Mai was lying, but why? What was she up to?

*   *   *

I walked toward journalism slowly. As the senior editor, I was supposed to introduce the vision for *The Bragg*

About this school year, and I was nervous. I had worked with Ms. Adams, the adviser, and I knew what I wanted to say, but I had never been the take-charge type. I was more comfortable writing articles, completing assignments, and leaving the vision and leadership to someone else. I had really thought I wanted to give it a try, but as I walked into the room I was having serious second thoughts.

The final bell rang, and Ms. Adams waved me up to the front of the room with her.

"Welcome to a new year, everybody. I'm your adviser, Ms. Adams, but *The Bragg About* belongs to you. You set the tone, you write the content, and you design the layout. I'm just here to help, so I'll turn it over to our new student editor, Beka Madison."

There was some unenthusiastic applause. I scanned the room and spotted Gretchen slumped in the corner at the bank of computers. Her usually curly hair was brushed straight and gathered at her neck with a gray scrunchie. She wore no makeup, and she looked like she had slept in her clothes. On the other side of the room, Mai was standing by the layout table with her arms crossed over her stomach and her weight shifted on one hip. With her Asian features and stylish dress she was a stark contrast to the fair Gretchen.

I cleared my throat. I tried to focus on the sophomores and juniors, the ones who seemed eager to hear what I was going to say.

"Hi. Well, I'm Beka. I'm not big on speeches, but I wanted to tell you what our theme is for the year, and then we have to get everybody assigned to the right area. So. We'll start with our theme."

I spent twenty minutes telling them all that Ms. Adams and I had discussed, and then I met with new students to see where they should work. It went fast, and except for Gretchen and Mai being there every day, I thought I might actually like doing it. Besides, it was bound to look good on a college application.

Near the end of the period I walked over to Gretchen. I was going to have to talk to her at some point. I wanted to get it over with. She had stayed at the same computer the entire period, barely looking up. She had her feet up on another chair and was using the mouse to look on the Internet.

"Hi." I stood off to the side.

She raised her head, looked at me, and then turned back to the computer screen. "What do you want?"

"Nothing. I, uh . . . Well, I thought we should . . ." Now that I was there I had nothing to say.

She glanced at me again. "So say what you came to say." She clicked on an image, and it sprang to life on the screen. I shifted my weight.

"Well, did you want to continue your column this year?" I clicked my pen and held it over my clipboard.

"No." She didn't look at me.

"Did you want to work on design and layout?"

"No."

I dropped my clipboard to my side.

"So what do you want to do?"

I waited for a full minute before I spoke again. "Gretchen?"

"What?" Her voice was barely a whisper.

"What should I put you down for?"

"I don't care." She clicked the mouse again and the screen went black. She stood up. "Do whatever you want." She walked past me, slid into one of the desks, and put her head down.

"Are you going to be able to work with her?" Ms. Adams appeared at my side.

I shrugged. "I don't think she wants to be here anyway."

"Probably not. But hang in there. She may need a friend before all is said and done."

I laughed. "A friend? Well, that wouldn't be me."

"You never know." Ms. Adams moved away, and I sat at a computer to type out the assignments. I just couldn't figure out what the year would hold.

Lucy wouldn't speak to me after school. It had been clear in journalism that at least part of what Mai had told Lucy was true. She and Gretchen did not seem to be friends. But I still didn't trust Mai. Every argument that I made to Lucy was met with an icy stare, and by the time I dropped her off at the gym I had given up. Lucy was going to do whatever Lucy wanted to do. No matter what I said.

I drove home and tried to turn my thoughts to Mark. As I pictured him, that warm honey feeling seeped into my chest. He really liked me. We couldn't date, but I could see him every day.

I grabbed the mail on the way in the house and

flipped through it. I stopped halfway up the stairs, turned, and sat down. There was a letter from Josh, with a Seattle postmark and my name across the front. I set my backpack down, laid the rest of the mail next to me, and slid my finger into the envelope.

Dear Beka,

I'm moved in and already buried in my classes. I thought I worked hard in high school, but this is a whole different ball game. My roommate is a guy named Gary. He and I do great together, and since he's really serious about his schoolwork, I think it will be a good year. I miss home though. And I think about you. How's your senior year going? I guess you just started, but I hope nobody's bothering you this year. I want you to be happy, so remember, I'll understand whatever you choose to do. Well, write me back if you can.

Josh

I read the note three times. Was he talking about me dating someone else? Or that he might? In Haiti he had said that I was to have "no obligation." What was I going to write back to him? I felt somewhat guilty about the situation with Mark. I had no reason to, but I still did. I wondered what Mark would think if he knew I was writing to Josh and what Josh would think about me holding hands with Mark. And then there was what my dad would think about any of it.

I walked up to my room after saying hi to Mary, the woman who helped out with the cooking and cleaning ever since my mom died. I pulled out some of the stationery Josh had gotten me for my birthday. I chose the kind with the tiny butterfly border and then stared at the paper.

> *Dear Josh,*
>
> *It was great to get your letter, and I'm glad things are good. We just started school today, so there's not much to tell yet. I have an appointment to meet with my guidance counselor to decide which colleges to apply to, but I still don't know what I should do. I'm hoping God gives me some sort of clue before they're due. What classes are you taking?*

I picked up my pen and chewed on it. Should I ask about girls? Fish a little bit for what he was thinking about? Then again, I didn't want him to feel obligated toward me if he didn't want to. I tapped the pen on my teeth and then finished the letter.

> *I have to say, it's strange being back here after Haiti. Sometimes I think my life is too complicated 'cause I make it that way. Everything was just simpler there. Work hard so you can eat so you can live. I don't ever have to worry whether there will be food for my sisters and me, which leaves me to worry about a hundred other things—which probably aren't that important anyway.*
>
> *I'm glad things are going well for you. I want you to be happy too.*
>
> *Beka*

I wasn't sure if I should write "take care" or "your friend" instead of just my name. I folded the letter and sealed it before I thought about it any longer. I didn't need any extra confusion in my life. Hadn't I just written that I worried too much about things that weren't important?

I plowed through my homework and went downstairs close to six for dinner. Anna was bouncing around, chattering about her day while we set the table, and Dad had picked Lucy up on his way home. It was still weird to not have Paul there.

"Girls?" Dad said when he walked in. He cleared his throat and avoided my eyes. "Gabby's coming over for dinner tonight. It was a last-minute thing. She'll be here soon. I'm going to go change and . . . yeah. I'll be right back."

"Goody, goody," Anna said. "I'll get 'nother plate."

Lucy walked by me but didn't say a word. I didn't need to deal with Gabby tonight. I finished setting the table and got last-minute directions from Mary as she gathered up her stuff to go home. Before Dad got back, though, there was a knock on the back door.

I opened it and tried to smile. I really did. But the minute I saw her I wanted to throw up. Her usually long, straight hair was now cropped to her shoulders, and she was actually wearing makeup. Instead of her barn uniform she was wearing a simple skirt and blouse. I almost didn't recognize her, but it was definitely her. I wanted to close the door in her face. Did she think this was some kind of date?

"Hey, Beka." Gabby smiled at me. "Haven't seen you in a while."

I moved aside to let her in. "Been busy."

"So I hear. Your dad said you got a job. Are you still doing that?"

"Not during the school year. Dad won't let me."

The silence thickened between us.

"Well, I need to get the rest of dinner ready." I moved toward the stove and reached for the pot holders.

Gabby dropped her purse in the corner of the kitchen. "Can I help with anything?"

"I've got it."

"Gabby!" Anna launched herself toward Gabby and wrapped her arms around her. "How's Wind Dancer? Is he doing okay?"

Gabby laughed gently. "He's great, kiddo. I fed him and turned him out just before I came here."

She didn't even smell like horses today. It was actual perfume. My stomach turned over. The thoughts tried to crowd in, and I kept trying to push them away. *This is not what it seems like. It's not. It can't be.*

"I wish Wind Dancer could live here. Then I could see him every day."

"I bet he misses you too. So how was school?" Gabby asked.

Anna told Gabby every detail of her day while I put the food on the table. Dad came in and said hi to Gabby, and I watched both of them like a hawk. What was going on? They exchanged glances but said nothing out of the ordinary. Lucy came in and fell into her chair.

"What's wrong?" Dad asked her as he pulled out a chair and sat down.

"Ask Beka," she said.

Dad looked at me for the first time since he walked in and raised his eyebrows at me. "She's mad at me because I don't want her hanging out with Mai."

"She can't choose my friends," Lucy said loudly.

"I told you. She was Gretchen's best friend. You can't trust her."

"I'm not you, Beka. I can handle myself."

"What's that supposed to mean?"

"Whoa. Whoa, girls. Let's stop this conversation for now. We have a guest. We'll talk about it later." Lucy bit her bottom lip and folded her arms. I sat down next to Anna. Gabby sat at the other end of the table from my dad. Where my mom used to sit. That's where Anna had put her plate, but it was still wrong.

Dad blessed the food and even asked for God to help Lucy and me resolve our differences. When he looked up, he cleared his throat.

"Everything looks great." He passed Anna her plate after slicing her a piece of lasagna. "I really like what you did with your hair, Gabby." He cleared his throat again and held out his hand for my plate, but he kept his eyes on Gabby.

"Thanks, Greg." She blushed and touched her hair.

The silence swept in as everybody began eating, but I couldn't do much more than push my food around my plate. Lucy didn't look like she was eating either. I felt sick. I knew exactly where this night was headed, and I just wanted to run away.

When we were halfway through the meal Dad cleared his throat again. Either he was getting sick or he was really nervous.

"Well, even though this was a last-minute thing, I thought it would be a good time to talk with you girls."

I stared at my dad. "Now? We have a guest, remember?"

"Well, that's why now is a good time."

"Greg?" Gabby drew her eyebrows together, asking a silent question.

Dad took a deep breath. "I wanted to let you girls know that Gabby and I are going to start seeing each other."

I tried to swallow the food in my mouth, but it wouldn't go past the lump in my throat.

"Seeing each other? Like you're going to date?" Lucy asked.

"Well. Yes. We're going to date."

"Are you going to be my new mom?" Anna's eyes were wide, and then her face melted into a grin. "That would be so cool."

I stared at my plate, unable to look up.

"No, Anna. Not right now. We just want a chance to get to know each other better," Dad told her.

"Are you planning on getting married?" Lucy asked the question I dreaded.

My dad paused way too long. "It's a little early to answer that. We want to date, spend some time together. See where God leads us."

I looked up in time to see him smile softly at Gabby. I stood up. I had to get out of there. "I need to be excused." I grabbed my plate and put it by the sink.

"Beka. Please stay."

I whirled around and faced Dad. "Why? You know exactly how I feel about this." I looked at Gabby. "No offense to you, but . . ." I couldn't form the words. I turned and left as my dad called after me. I went straight to my room and closed my door.

I dialed Lori's number in tears and told her what had happened.

"I'm sorry, Beka. I don't know what to say."

I sniffed and blew my nose. "This can't be happening."

Lori sighed.

"What's wrong?" I asked.

"Nothing. Why?"

"I don't know. You just sound weird."

"Oh. Well, it's nothing."

"You sound sad. Is everything okay with Brian?"

"Yeah, he's great."

"Then what is it?"

"Now's not a good time. You're upset, and I totally understand that."

"So something *is* wrong."

"It's not a big deal."

I heard a soft knock at my door. "Hold on, Lori. Come in."

Gabby poked her head around the corner and then moved to stand in my doorway.

"I've gotta go. I'll call you later."

I hung up the phone and straightened up on my bed.

"Can we talk?" she asked.

"I don't have anything to say." I tried not to sound snotty, but it came out that way anyway. Gabby pulled the chair over from my desk and sat down, smoothing down her skirt with both hands. She looked back up at me.

"I know you're not happy with me, but I hope we can have an adult conversation."

I grabbed a small butterfly pillow and pulled it into my lap. I shifted my shoulders away from her and squeezed the pillow.

"I don't have anything to say to you."

I glanced over at her, but she just sat, waiting.

I sighed loudly and turned away even more.

After at least five minutes of silence I turned and looked at her. "He told me you were just friends," I said.

"And we were. We are friends."

"Dating is different. He lied to me."

"No, he didn't. I don't think your dad ever really intended to date anyone after he lost your mom. He misses her a lot."

"If he did then he wouldn't be doing this. And why would you want to date him anyway? He loved my mom so much. He said he'd always love her."

"I would expect nothing less. Look, I'm not trying to replace your mom. I'm a completely different person."

"No kidding."

She sighed at my sarcastic comment but continued. "Beka. We are not trying to hurt you, but your dad and I do care about each other. We really want to follow God's lead, and we feel like this is the next step."

"You've wanted this from the beginning. You can't tell me that you would have been happy staying friends."

Gabby grew quiet. "I really care about your dad. I think I even love him. And I have for a long time. But it had to be his decision."

"You love him?" I spit the words out like they were maggots in my mouth. "Then this isn't about dating. You're gonna marry him. Aren't you? Aren't you?"

"One step at a time. Just because I feel something inside doesn't mean it's God's plan for me. We have to take it one step at a time. It's important for your dad and me, and important for you girls."

I looked away. "I don't want to talk about this anymore."

"Okay." I heard her stand up. "When you're ready, we'll talk again." I heard her close the door behind her as she left. I fell forward on my bed and let the tears come. I missed my mom so much. I felt like she was being betrayed, and I could do nothing to stop it.

I lay there till late and then wandered downstairs, hoping she was gone. I fixed a drink in the kitchen and sat at the counter to drink it.

"I thought I heard someone," Dad said. He came up and pressed his hands against the counter.

"I don't want to talk about it."

"We have to talk about it."

I looked at him. His eyes seemed sad. I couldn't bear the thought of him loving someone else. Kissing someone else. Sharing a bed and a life with someone else. The thought made me sick. I poked at the ice in my drink with my finger and then had a thought.

A very interesting thought.

"If you can date when I'm not happy about it, then I think you should let me date."

"You can date."

"I mean Mark."

"We talked about Mark."

"Yes, and we talked about Gabby too. You said she was just a friend."

"She was just a friend. And I came to you all when that began to change. Just like I promised."

"Well, I don't like her. And if you're going to date someone I don't like, then I should be allowed to date Mark."

Dad took a deep breath and paced around the island in the kitchen. He was actually considering it.

"Will you give Gabby a chance?"

"Will you give Mark a chance?"

"This isn't fair, Beka. This is blackmail."

"No, it's not. It's a deal, fair and square."

"You're forgetting that I'm the grown-up here. You're seventeen."

"Old enough to be given a chance. It's not like I'm thirteen anymore."

"I don't know if I trust Mark. Or you when you're with him."

"I feel the same way about Gabby."

Dad sighed. "I'll have to think about it some more. But I'll consider it. That's all I can promise. But no matter what I decide, I expect you to give Gabby a fighting chance. She's great. And I think you could like her."

I huffed. "I'll think about it."

Dad looked at me. "It was a lot easier when you were only thirteen, let me tell you."

"That's because Mom was around."

"Maybe." Dad smiled sadly. "So we'll talk more later?"

*   *   *

At least it was a chance.

CHAPTER 8

"For real?" Mark smiled and pulled me close. "That's the best news I've heard all day."

"It's only seven in the morning." I smiled back.

Lucy hadn't spoken to me at all, and Dad hadn't pushed us to resolve it because he was more worried about the Gabby announcement. If we hadn't been fighting about Mai I would have asked Lucy what she thought about it. I knew Anna was fine with it, but I wasn't positive about Lucy.

"It's only back under consideration. He hasn't said yes yet."

"But it's a possibility." He leaned in close to me but didn't kiss me. He had kept his word so far about not being too physical. But every time he didn't kiss me made me want him to kiss me more.

"I want to find Lori." I pulled him with me into the school. "And I like eating lunch with you, but lunch with Lori is like a girl thing."

"Are you telling me to butt out of your lunch?" He held his hand to his chest and stuck out his bottom lip. "I'm hurt."

I bumped into his shoulder. "Oh please. You understand, don't you?"

"I guess." He sighed heavily, and I walked up on my tiptoes and kissed him on the cheek. "Thanks for understanding."

He turned and grinned at me. "If I pout some more, will you kiss me again?"

"Don't push your luck."

"So I guess I'll see you in theory. Can I at least walk you there?"

"I suppose." I smiled at him. "See ya later."

I stopped by my locker and went to find Lori at hers. I waited for a few minutes before she came around the corner. She only half-smiled when she saw me.

"So what happened?" she asked.

"Gabby came upstairs to talk with me. But I got Dad to consider letting me date Mark if I will give Gabby a chance."

"You think he'll go for it?"

"I don't know." I leaned against the locker. "What's up with you?"

Her porcelain skin and dark hair always made her

look like a knockout, but her green eyes looked red and puffy.

She sighed. "It's nothing."

"Liar."

She swung around and looked at me.

"I'm just teasing you. Sorry," I said.

She closed her locker. "I don't think I should say anything."

"It's me, remember?"

"I know. But it's not me, really. If it was my secret I'd tell you in a minute, but . . ." Her eyes teared up and a tear fell on her cheek.

"Lori, what is it?"

"I can't." She turned and walked down the hallway, leaving me standing there alone.

*　　*　　*

At lunch Lori wouldn't talk about whatever was bothering her, but she seemed a little better. She even thanked me for tossing Mark from our lunch table. Mark was standing just past the freshman quad, so as soon as Lori left for class, Mark came up and took my hand.

"Hey there, Beautiful," he said.

I grinned but said nothing. When we got to class he sat next to me until Thompson called him into the office to file some papers, and then Thompson returned with a stack of papers.

"First order of business." Thompson handed out the papers, tossing them to the kids sitting closest to him. We were sitting on random chairs, couches, and stools scattered across the room. I grabbed the stack that was tossed on my lap, took one, and passed the stack to a boy sitting next to me. He looked scared. Had to be a freshman.

I looked at the paper. It had "Semester Project" written across the top in all caps, and it had three different deadlines and a list of possible projects.

"You have until Christmas break to complete this project. I expect you to start thinking about it today. I expect it to be brilliant."

He paced the room, stopping to stare at us every so often. "I've put down some projects you could consider, but whatever you choose I want a proposal in to me by the end of next week. Got it?" We all gave him a wide-eyed nod. I looked over and saw Mark grinning at me from T's office doorway. He winked at me and then disappeared back inside.

T slapped his hands together, making the room give a collective jump. "So let's get started on structure."

*   *   *

Mark met me at the door when the bell rang.

"Did you know about this?" I asked.

Mark shrugged. "Sure. T does it every year. I took theory at my last high school though. Not with T."

"Do you know what he means by 'perform'? I was thinking I'd try this one—'compose and perform an original song'—but where would we perform it?"

"It would be a Friday night show. Part of the holiday concert. I think the show choir, the performing arts club, and the jazz band all perform, and then there's a section for performance projects. Haven't you ever been?"

I shook my head. I loved the idea of writing my own song, but performing it? In front of the school?

"You were Annie, Beka. The holiday concert would be no big deal."

"But that was a part in a play. I had a costume and makeup. This would be just me, walking out on stage all by myself." I shook my head. "I don't know."

"Well, is there something else there?" Mark took the paper and leaned against a locker outside my next class.

"Sure, but nothing I could do. I mean, like I'm going to organize a band? Right."

"I had a band."

"I'm sure you did. But I'm not the band type."

He smiled at me and pulled me close. "You've got the prettiest eyes."

I felt my cheeks get hot. "I better go inside."

He took a deep breath and let it out slowly. He winked and walked away, and I went into my classroom, positive that my feet weren't touching the ground.

*　　*　　*

We began work on our back-to-school issue in journalism. Gretchen tucked herself in the corner computer station as soon as she walked in, and watching her it was hard to believe she was the same girl I had dreaded seeing every single day. I figured the best thing to do was just stay away from her.

I was talking with Sabrina, a smart and eager junior,

about the layout for the first page when Mai came up and tossed a small stack of papers at me on the table. Sabrina and I both sat back and looked at her.

"You have to sign off on my article, Miss Editor."

"It's done already?" I tried to smile, but it came out awkward and I felt goofy. I stood up. "Thanks, I'll look it over."

Mai didn't move. She cast her eyes down on Sabrina until Sabrina shifted uncomfortably, cleared her throat, and then left, muttering about getting some papers. Mai looked back at me with her face still frozen.

"I expect you to sign off on that." She jutted her chin toward the paper.

"Well." I nodded at her. "I'll give it a look. What is it anyway?"

"It's my new column."

"What?" I looked down at the paper and then back at her, feeling confused.

"I took over Gretchen's column. That's not a problem, is it?"

"Well, I . . . I mean we . . . Gretchen didn't want to do it, so Ms. Adams and I cut the column." I clenched my jaw and looked between the paper and Mai. "You were assigned to features, right? Isn't that what you wanted to do?"

Mai lifted her right eyebrow just slightly. "That's my article. I suggest you sign off on it." Mai turned away, and I fell back into my chair. It was only the second day of school.

*   *   *

78

"Lucy, please can we talk about this?" I glanced over at her as we drove to the gym after school.

"For the millionth time, you can't choose my friends."

"I'm just trying to help. Mai is not safe. I know she's up to something."

"You're paranoid." Lucy turned away from me.

Maybe I was being paranoid.

"It's just weird, that's all. There's no reason for her to be hanging out with you except to get to me."

"So I'm not cool enough to hang out with?" Lucy scowled at me.

"You're a freshman. She's a senior."

"So?"

"So it's not normal. I'm telling you, she's up to something."

"She wants me to join the cheerleading squad. She says I'd be awesome at it since I can tumble and I'm little enough to be a flier."

"Like you have time for that. You're at the gym every day."

She shrugged.

"Are you seriously considering it?" I pulled into the Paragon Gymnastics parking lot and put the car in park.

"Why not?"

"Because you're a gymnast. It's what you've always done."

Lucy opened the door and climbed out. "Well, maybe it's time for something different." She slammed the door, tossed her gym bag over her shoulder, and disappeared into the gym. I leaned back against the seat and blew out a long, slow breath.

* * *

"You can't let her quit, Dad. You've got to talk to her." I had pulled my dad into the family room as soon as he got home. He pulled his tie out and undid the top button of his shirt.

"I'll talk to her. But why does this upset you so much?"

"Because she's worked so hard. And she's going to throw it all away because Mai told her she'd be good at cheerleading. Of course she'd be good at it. She'd probably be the best one on the squad. But she can't give up gymnastics, everything she's worked for."

Dad looked at me, but I couldn't read his expression.

"What?" I asked.

He shook his head. "I'll talk to her. But Beka, be her sister; don't try to be her mom. Okay?"

"I am trying to be a sister here. I know you think I'm being paranoid, but Mai is trouble. I am just trying to help. Make sure she doesn't get hurt."

Dad shook his head. "I've heard you, okay?"

I rolled my toes into the carpet, debating whether I should bring up Mark. I knew I should probably wait for him to bring it up, but I couldn't resist.

"Umm. Have you thought any more about Mark?" I ventured.

Dad closed his eyes for a long second and then shook his head. "Sorry, Butterfly. I need some more time on that one. I happen to feel the same way about Mark as you do about Mai."

"Huh? You can't be serious. I want to date. I'm not trying to throw away my future."

"Dating can sometimes alter our future, though."

"Are you considering it, or have you already made up your mind?"

"I could ask you the same question about Gabby."

I felt my chest tighten at the sound of her name.

"If you'll think and pray, then I promise I'll do the same," he said.

*　　*　　*

I walked up to my room and crawled onto my bed. I didn't want to think about Gabby. I could see my Bible on my bedside table, but I shifted to look in the opposite direction. I knew what it would say. Love your enemies. Love your neighbors. Blah, blah, blah. The question was how to do that. How was I supposed to love someone I couldn't stand? Even Mai wasn't as hard to cope with, because she wasn't trying to become a permanent part of my life. In one more year, I'd probably never see Mai again. I smiled at that thought. But Gabby. If she married Dad . . . I turned over and picked up the Bible and laid it in front of me.

I knew I wasn't in a good place. And if God was going to help me out of it, I was going to have to at least try.

I flipped it open and began to read.

It's up to you, Beka. As long as it's appropriate for the paper, then it's your call." Ms. Adams put her clipboard down on the desk and took off her glasses.

I looked down at Mai's column in my hand. I had read it at least five times. It was a lot like the column Gretchen used to do with movie star gossip, fashion trends, and such. The article was okay, but what bothered me was an entire section about a young, lesser-known star who had stayed in a psychiatric hospital for a while. Who would care about something like that? And it made me wonder if that section was meant as a dig at me.

Mai knew I had stayed at a psychiatric hospital last Christmas. I was sure Gretchen had told her. But other than Lori, no one else at school knew, and I really wanted to keep it that way. Gretchen didn't seem to care about spreading my secret anymore, but with Mai staring at me with daggers in her eyes, I knew I wasn't safe.

I moved back to my desk in the corner, a nice big teacher-sized desk, and sank into my chair. I could be imagining things, but it seemed so off for Mai to bring that up other than to let me know that she knew. I felt my stomach flip over. I couldn't bear for Mark to know about it. He actually liked me. I didn't want him to think I was mentally unstable.

I looked up and saw Mai across the room talking with Liz, another of Gretchen's former group. As if she knew I was staring at her, Mai looked over at me and caught my eye. She turned and said something to Liz and then sauntered toward me. I took a deep breath. I had nothing to fear. Right? After all, I was in charge.

"You done with that?" Mai jutted her chin at her column. "I need to get it to layout."

"Almost. We need to, um, talk about it."

"Really?" Mai planted her hands on her hips and shifted her weight to her left hip.

"Yeah. If you want to do the column, that's fine. It's just . . ." I hesitated. *Could I make things worse by pointing it out?* I slid the paper over to her and squared my shoulders. "It's just Bryce Abrams is a nobody, and you spend half your article on him."

I picked up another article and began to read it, hoping Mai would take the hint. I could tell she was still standing there, so I glanced back up. "Anything else?" I asked.

Mai picked up the papers. "I think Bryce's mental problems are exactly what people want to know about. It's fascinating material." She paused. "Don't you think?"

"Not particularly. But if you want to leave it in, go ahead."

Mai smirked and walked away, and I let out the breath I was holding. The year stretched out in front of me. I didn't know if I had the energy to worry about Mai every day.

*   *   *

Mark was waiting outside of my class when I walked out juggling my backpack and a stack of papers. His smile sent my heart skittering.

"Let me take those." He took the papers, brushing his arms against mine as he did, and the gooseflesh on my arms joined my thumping heart. Why did he do that to me?

"Thanks. You're the sweetest," I said.

He shot me a grin. "So what are you doing this weekend?"

"Lori's coming over tonight. We're going to see a movie." I glanced over at him and watched him raise his eyebrows.

"Any word from your dad yet?"

I shook my head. "He's still considering it."

"Why don't you just tell him you'll lay off of Gabby, and then you and I can be together? Officially."

"I don't want her marrying my dad."

"He might marry her anyway."

My heart sank in my chest. Of course that was true. I'd be leaving for college, hopefully, in a year. If Dad wanted to marry her, he probably wasn't going to let me stand in their way.

I unlocked my car door, and Mark put my papers in the backseat and then put his hands on my waist. "Did I upset you?"

"Only because you're right."

The corners of his lips drew down. He brushed a piece of hair away from my face and then let his hand slide down my cheek. He leaned closer until his forehead rested on mine.

"Can I help?" he asked.

"How? There's nothing I can do."

"Give up on Gabby. Then at least we could be together." He kissed me gently on the lips and pulled away. "Sorry. I couldn't resist."

"You're not sorry." I pushed his shoulder.

He laughed. "You're right." He leaned in and stole another kiss. "Lori's coming."

I turned and looked over my shoulder and saw Lori walking across the parking lot. I was pretty sure she saw us.

"I'm worried about her too," I said when I turned back to him.

"What's up?"

"I'm not sure. She doesn't want to talk about it. But she's so sad." I didn't want to say any more. Lori came up and stopped at the passenger door. "I better go."

"I'll see you later." Mark pointed and winked at me. "Bye, Lori."

Lori lifted her hand and waved, then climbed into the car.

*   *   *

Lori had looked sad all week and still would not tell me what was bothering her. She walked as if the world were sitting on her shoulders, and her usual glow was dull and faded. She gave me a half smile as she closed her door.

"I know what you're thinking," I said. I started the car and shifted it into drive.

"No, you don't," she said. "I was just thinking how cute you two look together."

My heart felt full to the brim. "You think?"

She nodded. "I miss Brian."

We drove to my house in silence. I couldn't do anything to help her, and I didn't want to talk about Mark when the guy she liked was nearly four hours away at school.

When we got to my room, I pointed at my bed. We both settled in with a pillow. "Now what gives? Why are you so sad lately?"

She dropped her head and ran her finger along the butterfly embroidered on the pillow. When she looked back up, tears were already falling from her eyes.

"What is it?"

"I don't think I can even say it."

"Lori. I won't say anything. I promise. You need to talk to someone. What about Megan?"

Fear washed over her features, and she shook her head quickly.

What could it be that she couldn't even talk to Megan? I waited.

We sat for at least twenty minutes with Lori crying softly and me wondering how far to push her. I didn't want to pry, but I didn't want her to be all alone in whatever she was facing. I wanted to be a friend. She had stuck by me through so many things.

After a while she whispered, "It's David, my dad."

"What about him?"

She looked up at me, her eyes puffy and red and desperate. "You won't say anything? You have to swear that you won't tell anybody."

I lifted my right hand. "I swear."

Her body shuddered as she let out her breath. "I don't even know where to start." She closed her eyes. "He didn't know that I was home. Megan dropped me off early so that she could take Kari Lynn to a doctor's appointment. I didn't know he was home."

I leaned back on the headboard and watched Lori struggle to put words to her thoughts. Megan and David Rollins had just adopted Lori early this year, and she had been so happy until recently. From the outside, they looked like the perfect little family.

"I walked into the study, and he was watching something on the computer. When he saw me he wiped the screen and yelled at me for walking in."

I couldn't see what the big deal was. "What was he watching? Did you see?"

Lori nodded slowly. "It was, you know, some porno

thing. Only it wasn't just pictures, it was like a movie but on the computer." Lori's face was contorted in disgust.

"What?"

"That horrible image. I just can't get it out of my head." The words came out in a hoarse whisper, and she dropped her eyes down to the bed. "It was so awful."

"When was this?"

"It was during the summer. Late July, I guess."

I tried to put it all together. "It's still bothering you?"

She sighed. "He keeps doing it. I've seen him in there at least three other times and then last night."

"Oh, Lori. That's so . . . gross." I thought about how I would feel if I found my dad like that. I couldn't even let the picture form in my head without pushing it away in horror. "Is it the same thing every time?"

"Pretty much, but he didn't know I saw again until last night. He was really mad."

"What did he say?"

"He yelled at me about privacy and all that. He said to keep my mouth shut. But it wasn't just what he said. It was the way he looked at me. Like I was an intruder. I don't even feel like I should be in that house anymore."

"Oh, Lori. Why didn't you tell me sooner? I hate that I haven't been there for you."

"At first I thought maybe this is some normal thing. My real dad died when I was so young, and the guys my mom had around were all sleazy and drunk. I thought because my new mom and dad were Christians there wouldn't be this kind of stuff going on. I just don't know how to deal with him anymore. He knows I know, and so it's been weird when he's home. I think Mom suspects something is wrong. After last night, I was so glad to come to school and then over here. He's just so mad at me, and I don't know what to do."

I took a deep breath. I had no idea what to tell her. I remembered that one of the elders in our church several years ago was removed because he was using Internet pornography. It was a big mess, lots of people were upset, and for a while they talked about the dangers of pornography almost every week. Every once in a while the topic still came up. Lori's church was a lot smaller than mine, but Megan and David were leaders there, and if they found out what David was doing, it could be a big mess for them too.

But Lori couldn't just pretend nothing happened, could she?

"Thanks for letting me vent. I feel a little better."

"What are you gonna do?" I asked.

"Nothing. What can I do? If I say something, he could get in trouble at church, and Mom—she'd be devastated. I can't do that to them."

"So you're just going to keep it a secret?"

"I have no choice. Maybe if I talk to him, tell him I won't say anything, maybe then he won't be so mad at me."

I shook my head. This one felt like deep water to me, and I didn't know how to swim there.

*   *   *

We decided to go ahead and go to the movies since we needed something fun to do. Dad gave me some money, and we went early so we could hang out at The Fire Escape, a little coffee and ice cream shop across the street from the movie theater. We ordered some Cappuccino Chillers and found a seat on the patio. Lots of kids from school were there, but no Mai, so I relaxed and decided that I'd do everything I could to get Lori's mind off her problems with her dad.

But before I even had a chance to start a conversation, I looked through the window of the café and saw Mark at the counter paying for something. Every nerve in my body came to alert. Then I saw Brian standing next to him. I looked at Lori and then back at Mark and Brian as they walked toward us. Mark smiled at me when he caught my eye.

"You are never going to believe who's here," I said.

"Who?" Lori turned around in her chair. She jumped up and ran for Brian. Mark came and sat beside me while Lori and Brian hugged. After a few minutes of a hushed conversation, they walked over and sat down with us.

"You did this?" Lori asked Mark.

"Guilty," he said.

"Somebody want to fill me in?" I asked.

"Mark called me at school this afternoon and said I needed to come home this weekend. That Lori needed some cheering up," Brian said.

"Did he really?" I looked at Mark, who had a sheepish grin on his face. I shook my head. I knew exactly what he was up to. "And you guys just happened to come to the movies tonight, huh?"

"Thanks, Mark. I owe you one." Lori laid her head on Brian's shoulder.

"Be careful. I may take you up on that. Besides, I had to show you I wasn't such a bad guy," he said.

"I don't think you're a bad guy," Lori protested.

Mark lifted his eyebrows.

"Well, you just keep getting Beka in trouble."

"We'll behave. I promise."

Lori looked up at Brian and then back at Mark. "Then I'll give you another chance. I guess you deserve at least that."

Mark took my hand under the table and rubbed it. "So, should we go see a movie?"

It was so great to sit and watch the movie with Mark holding my hand and whispering in my ear. Every time the lead actress flipped her hair over her shoulder he said, "Oh, I'm so pretty." I giggled through the whole movie. Lori snuggled with Brian a row in front of us. Mark thought they should have some privacy. We stayed out till the last possible second, and then Lori and I drove back to my house.

"He's not leaving until Sunday, so I'll see if I can go with him somewhere tomorrow," Lori said as we climbed into bed. "Mark's incredible for doing that. I don't think I ever would have called Brian to ask him to come back here."

"Why not?"

"'Cause he would come. And I would feel bad for making him miss time to study, be with friends. You know." She smiled. "But no guilt tonight. I'm so glad he's here."

I shut out the light, and I watched the shadow of the ceiling fan spin in slow circles above our heads.

"Maybe I've been hard on Mark," Lori said. "I can see why you like him so much."

"Yeah."

"Have you heard from Josh?" she asked.

"Mm-hm. I got a letter, and I wrote back to him. It's weird. I'm not sure I see the point. I know he's going to fall in love with someone out there." I punched my pillow and settled in. "And maybe he should."

"Do you really believe that?"

I let the silence linger until I felt like I didn't have to answer. Because I wasn't sure what I believed.

I drove Lori home early so that she could spend the day with Brian.

"Is there anyone you could talk to? Maybe at your church?" I asked. I still felt bad that she had told me her big secret about her dad, and I didn't have one good piece of advice.

"No way. They'd ask him about it, and he'd know I told."

"What about my dad?"

"Beka, you promised."

"I'm not going to tell him. I'm saying you could talk to him if you want. He might know what to do."

"I'll think about it. Later, though. Because today

Brian's in town." She climbed out of the car and waved from the porch. I backed out and wondered what Mark was up to.

*   *   *

Dad was in the kitchen drinking a cup of coffee at the counter when I walked in.

"Lori has other plans today?" he asked.

"Yeah, her boyfriend is in town for the weekend. He goes to Tech."

Even though I had emphasized the word *boyfriend*, Dad only nodded.

"How did your first week of school go?"

I pulled over a stool and climbed on. "Not bad. I like being the editor. Mostly."

"Mostly?" He looked at me over his mug.

"Mai is in the class. She's being kind of difficult. Did you talk to Lucy about that?"

Dad nodded. "She assures me there's nothing to worry about."

I huffed.

"She hasn't decided yet about the cheerleading, so let's give her a bit of space."

"Whatever." I jumped off the stool.

"Before you go. We've got plans tonight. Luce is in the gym until noon, and Anna comes back from her sleepover around then, so I thought we'd all go out to lunch and then go bowling or play some golf. Whatever you girls want to do."

I narrowed my eyes at him. "Just the four of us?"

He coughed. "Well, I thought Gabby could come along. She only has a half day of riding lessons today."

I walked toward the door.

"Beka. Is that okay with you?"

"No, but it doesn't matter, 'cause you're going to make me go and spend time with her. Aren't you?" My voice cracked, and I felt the tears burning in my eyes. "You make me sit around and wait for an answer about Mark even though you and Gabby are going to do whatever *you* want to do. It's not fair. I should have a say. This is my family too."

I tore out of the room before he could stop me and went to my bedroom. Lori was with Brian, so I dialed Mark's cell number. If I hadn't been upset I wouldn't have had the nerve to do it.

"Yeah."

"Mark? It's Beka."

"Hey, Beautiful."

"What are you doing today?"

"Not much. Why? Can you come out and play?"

I let a small laugh slip out. "I wish. But maybe tonight. I have an idea."

"You've got my attention."

"Can I call you later? See if it works out?"

"I'll be here. Just call me on this number."

"Okay. Bye." I hung up feeling just a little better. Now I just had to make a plan.

*   *   *

I went downstairs before noon, dressed and ready to go. When Dad saw me he smiled.

"You okay, Butterfly?"

I shrugged. I had to play this right. "I think if I have to spend the entire afternoon doing something I don't want to do to make you happy, then I should be able to go out tonight."

Dad drew his eyebrows together. "First of all, I don't like that attitude."

"It will get a lot better if you'd just give me a chance."

"Where do you want to go? Or should I ask, who do you want to go with?"

"Mark."

Dad sighed. "I don't know, Beka."

"It's no big deal. You act like I'm going to run off and marry him or something crazy like that. It's just a date!" My voice rose, and Dad reacted by clenching his jaw.

"Look. I feel like you're going to do whatever you want, regardless of how I feel about it. Wait." I put up my hand as he started to protest. "It's my senior year of high school. Why can't you at least give me this?"

Dad's eyes softened, and he sat down on the closest stool. He didn't say anything for several minutes, and I could feel my short, nervous breaths drawing tighter across my chest as the minutes ticked by.

Finally, he looked up. "Is it that important to you?"

"Yes," I pleaded.

"All right. But I want to know where you're going, and you are to be back no later than eleven o'clock."

"You let me stay out till eleven thirty last night."

"Fine, eleven thirty. But not a minute later."

"Thank you!" I squealed and ran over and hugged him. "I promise I'll try to be nice to Gabby today."

"You better," he said.

*   *   *

But that was easier said than done. Lunch was okay because Anna and Lucy spent most of the time talking, so I was able to just sit and smile politely. But when we got to the bowling lanes, Gabby sat down next to me, and Anna and Lucy weren't there to rescue me.

"So I heard you have a date tonight."

I nodded, but inside I seethed. It was none of her business. Why was Dad telling her things like that?

"Is this the same guy you were with out at the farm?"

"Yeah." I laced up my ugly bowling shoes again. Tighter.

"He was cute. Mark, right?"

"Mm-hmm."

"Beka. I wanted to talk to you about your dad and me."

I sat up. "I'm not sure why I should believe anything you say. You told me you were just friends too. You both lied to me."

She shook her head. "No. The minute we thought it was more, we told you girls."

"So are you going to marry him?"

She flinched. "It's too soon to say."

"Do you want to marry him?"

Another flinch. "If that's where God leads it, yes."

"God, huh? I guess how I feel doesn't matter."

"It does matter. A lot. I wish I could prove to you how much I care. That I'm not trying to replace your mom." She paused and pulled at her slacks. She was dressed up again, looking very different from the barn woman I first met. But underneath the new haircut and silk blouse I knew it was the same woman trying to hone in on my family.

She continued, "You're seventeen, Beka. You're not a child anymore. You'll probably be going away to college, getting married someday, and making a family of your own. Do you really expect your dad to live the rest of his life alone—missing your mom?"

The images she suggested paraded across my mind, showing me leaving first, then Lucy and Anna, and then my dad all by himself. And all of a sudden I felt selfish. And mean. I glanced over at Gabby sitting next to me. I had known for a long time that she loved my father. Maybe not the same way my mom did, but she did love him. And Dad was happy with her. Was it fair for me to deny him that?

Fortunately, Dad called me over to take my turn, and we never got back to the conversation. Around three thirty I started watching the big Coca-Cola clock on the back wall. Mark was supposed to pick me up at four, and my dad had insisted he stay for a few minutes. Mark didn't seem to mind when I told him on the phone, but I wished we could avoid the family scene. It was a little embarrassing. You never knew what Anna might say.

I watched Mark stroll in just after four and glance around the alley, and then he locked eyes with me. He made his way over to our lane and approached my dad with his hand out.

"Mr. Madison."

"Mark."

They nodded at each other.

"Are you Beka's boyfriend?" Anna asked. She danced around in front of the ball return.

Mark laughed. "Why? Do you have a boyfriend?"

"Noooo." She snorted. "But Joey Thadren likes me."

"How do you know?" Mark sat down on one of the molded chairs, and Anna climbed onto the one next to him and gave him all the dirt on her fourth-grade class.

Dad looked at me. "It's your turn, Butterfly."

I picked up the purple ball I was using, lined up my shot, and let the ball go in one fluid motion. One thing I did know how to do was bowl. We went all the time as a family, less since my mom died, but Dad seemed to be trying to reinstate the tradition.

"You two can go along if you want. Don't forget your curfew," Dad said after we had finished up the game we were working on.

"Cool." I unlaced my shoes. Mark walked over to my dad.

"Thanks for giving us a chance."

Dad squared his shoulders and looked down at Mark, who was a few inches shorter than he was. "That's my baby. You watch out for her."

"Daaa-ad." I felt my cheeks flush, and Gabby let a small laugh escape from her mouth.

I grabbed my bag, and Mark and I made our exit as soon as he had said good-bye to Anna and Lucy.

"So where to?" Mark asked as he pulled out of the parking lot.

"Food. I'm starving."

Mark reached over and took my hand. "It's our first official date, you know."

"I know. Now that we've got the okay from everybody. You said your parents are fine with it, right?"

"Mostly."

I turned and looked at him. "You said your parents had changed their minds."

"They did, but they're not happy about it."

"Great."

"It's not you. They're still trying to trust me. It was hard enough for them to deal with the idea that I had gotten Chelsea pregnant, but when she lost the baby, they lost their grandchild. It's been hard on them. And I'm not about to put them through that again."

"I'm glad to hear that," I said.

*   *   *

After a great dinner and a movie we ended up at The Fire Escape, which was swarming with teenagers by that point. It felt different that night being with Mark, mostly because I was allowed to be there. I wanted everybody to see us there as a couple, to make it official, not that kids at school hadn't already seen us that way.

We were talking about my music theory project when a couple of guys I recognized, but didn't know well, came up to Mark.

"Hey, man. What's up?" They slapped hands and pulled out chairs.

"Not now, man, I'm with my girl," Mark said.

"That's cool. Can you hook us up with a ride over to Angela's Party?"

Mark looked at me, then back at the two guys. "Give me a minute, okay?" They moved away and started hitting on a couple of girls at the counter.

"Would you mind, Beka? They look like they've already been partying."

"It's okay. You want me to wait here for you?"

"No. Come with me. Maybe we'll drive out and take a walk on the beach."

I shuddered. I hadn't been back to the beach since my attack, and the thought of Bonfire Beach brought images crashing like waves through my mind.

"All right."

The two guys, who I found out were Devon and Travis, climbed into the tiny backseat. It took about ten minutes to get there. The party was going full blast. Angela and I had a class together, so I knew her a little bit. She was pretty nice, even though she was popular. Of course, not quite as popular as Gretchen used to be, but still well liked.

Mark got out to let them crawl out his side and then leaned down and spoke into the window. "I'm going to go in for a minute. Do you want to wait out here?"

I looked around. We were at the end of a cul-de-sac, and I couldn't see but one other house. It was really dark, and there were cars scattered up and down the street. I wasn't about to sit there by myself.

"I'm coming with you," I said, climbing out. I was his girl.

I followed Mark into the enormous foyer deep into a sea of bodies. I grabbed a loop of his pants so I wouldn't get lost in all the chaos. The music throbbed around me, and the stale air was ripe with sweat and beer. He led me out onto a patio, which helped me breathe a little better since the crush of people was less intense and there was considerably more air.

I fell into a patio chair that was covered with a bright red cushion while Mark stood next to me scanning the backyard.

"I don't see them. Beka, do you mind waiting here? I just want to check on a couple of friends. Is that okay?"

"Sure. I'll be fine." It was a nice night, and as long as I could stay outside I felt good.

"Do you want me to get you something?" He knelt by my chair and laid his arm across mine.

"No, I'm fine."

"Okay. I'll be back." He kissed my cheek and then disappeared back inside the house. I looked around at all the kids gathered in clusters around the patio and backyard. A pool shimmered in the yard below, but no one was swimming. Probably because it was too chilly. The house was surrounded by woods, and the music echoed into the darkness. I shifted back toward the kitchen and what I could see of the party through the French doors that were flung wide open. I watched the sea of bodies lift and fall in time with the music.

I wondered where Mark had gone off to. As the time passed I became antsier. Since I didn't have a watch on, I didn't know if it had been fifteen or fifty minutes that we had been there.

"No way! It's freezing out here!" a voice yelled below me.

"Come on!"

"You have to do it."

I leaned over the railing to see what the commotion was and saw a group of kids moving toward the swimming pool. I laughed, glad that it wasn't me about to be thrown into a pool. They pushed a girl forward, and she stumbled toward the pool but stopped at the very edge. She turned and looked back at the group, a light shining on her face.

It was Lucy.

Before I could even react, someone stepped forward and shoved her in, but she pulled whoever it was in with her. Lucy's head bobbed up, followed by Mai's face.

I ran down the stairs onto the lower patio by the pool and looked at the group. Theresa and Liz were there, two more of Gretchen's former friends. As far as I could tell, Mai seemed to be in charge of the group. Jeremy, Lance, Ethan, and Chrissy were standing around laughing at Mai. Then I saw Amy, Lucy's best friend, leaning over the edge of the pool to help Lucy out. Mai crawled out of the pool, and before I could say anything she took her foot and shoved Amy headfirst into the pool as well. A roar of laughter went up from the group.

"You can get out now. Your baptism is over with." Mai leaned her head back and laughed at her own cleverness. Then she saw me. Her face immediately went cold, and she crossed her arms across her belly.

"What are you doing here?"

"I'm with Mark. What is she doing here?" I pointed at Lucy, who had climbed out and was now shivering with Amy at the edge of the pool with a look of panic in her eyes.

"We invited her." Mai looked around at the group and smiled.

"I told you to stay away from her." I felt severely outnumbered, and I could feel a crowd growing around me. Where was Mark when I needed him?

Mai snorted. "I think you've got it backwards. *You* need to stay away from her. You don't want to contaminate this girl. She could actually be popular. I never thought there was a Madison who could be. Surprise, surprise."

I turned to Lucy. "We're leaving."

She stood frozen.

"You don't have to go anywhere, Lucy. The night is young." Mai turned back to me. "But I think maybe you ought to be running along home. Buh-bye." She waved her hand, and the group turned and went back into the lower level of the house. Amy and Lucy, dripping wet, followed them in. Lucy cast a look at me but didn't stop.

I didn't know what to do. I couldn't just leave my little sister at a party that was way out of her league. She didn't know how to handle herself. Was she drinking? What was I going to tell my dad? Should I tell him?

I wandered back up onto the porch and started looking for Mark. Maybe he would have some advice or an idea on what I should do about Lucy. I went through the kitchen and into the living room at the pace of an old woman with crutches. There were so many people. Some I recognized; some I didn't. A few guys tried to dance with me as I walked across the middle of the living room, but I moved away as quickly as I could manage. I didn't see Mark anywhere, and I wasn't tall enough to see over everybody. I looped back into the foyer and found the stairs to the basement. I went down the stairs and scanned the rec room, noticing Lucy and Amy on the couch. Ethan Sands had his arm around Lucy. I wanted to go drag him off of her, but I couldn't get her out of there unless I found Mark. I checked every room and then went back outside and up the deck stairs and back into the kitchen to try the other direction.

By that time I was tired and irritated, and I just wanted to get out of there. Not to mention I had a curfew, and I knew it must be getting late. On the way through the kitchen I checked the digital clock on the stove. It glowed 11:25, and I gasped. Even if I left that minute I was going to be late. I had no cell phone, and I couldn't call from the house because Dad would hear the party.

I wanted to scream.

Then I spotted Mark over by the window in the dining room with a can of Dr. Pepper in his hands, laughing and talking with a couple of guys.

I came up next to him with a scowl on my face. He stopped laughing. "What's wrong?"

"Would you excuse us?" I asked the two guys. They lifted their hands, snickering at Mark. Mark waved good-bye. "Do you know what time it is?"

He glanced at his watch. "I guess we better go."

"Ya think? We're going to be late. That means this might be our first and last date."

"I lost track of time. I'm sorry."

"I'm going to get Lucy. I'll meet you at the car."

"Lucy?"

"Yeah. Promise me you'll be there."

"I'll go now. Do you need help?"

"No, just go to the car." I managed to get to the basement again and told Amy and Lucy they were coming with me. Lucy protested, but they followed me up the stairs and into Mark's car.

"You can't take me home. Dad knows I'm spending the night with Amy. He'll know where I went."

"Of course he will, because you're going to tell him."

"Please, just take me to Amy's. You can't do this to me!"

I turned around in my seat. Amy was cowering in the backseat, and Mark was silent.

"Lucy, you did this to yourself."

"Come on, Beka. Be my sister. Cover for me."

I huffed and leaned back on my seat. "What am I supposed to do?" I felt like bursting into tears. First Mark abandons me at a party, and then Lucy ends up being there. *Be her sister.* That's what my dad had said too. What would a sister do? I looked at my watch. If we took them to Amy's I was going to be at least thirty minutes late for curfew.

"Mark. I need your phone."

Mark flipped open his phone.

I dialed and took a deep breath.

"Dad? It's Beka."

"You're late. You ask for another chance, and you break curfew."

"I'll be home as quickly as I can."

"I want you home now." I could tell Dad was angry.

I glanced back at Lucy and frowned at her. "I'm on my way." I hung up the phone and handed it back to Mark. "Take a right here. We'll take them to Amy's."

"Thank you. Thank you, Beka!"

I whirled around in my seat. "I'm late because of you, and if Dad grounds me I'll . . . I'll . . ." I turned back around and buried my face in my hands. I felt Mark's hand on my back, but instead of feeling sweet, it made me mad. "Where were you? You just left me there. Do you know what's going to happen when I get home?"

"Don't worry. I'll explain it to him."

"Like that will help." I turned and looked out the

window, giving Mark directions to Amy's. After we dropped Lucy and Amy off, we left for my house and pulled into the driveway at 12:03.

"Do you want me to come in with you?" Mark asked.

"No. It'll just make it worse." I climbed out and closed the door. Mark came around and reached for me. "And that will definitely make it worse. I'm sure he's watching."

Mark took a deep breath. "I'll call you tomorrow."

I lifted my hand in a halfhearted wave and went toward the back stairs. I wanted to just sit on the back porch and get my bearings before I went in, but I didn't want to be any later than I already was. Dad was sitting at the kitchen table, waiting for me.

"Sit."

I felt the tears start even before I made it to the chair. This wasn't my fault, and it was all going to come down on my head.

"Start explaining." He drummed his fingers on the table, and his eyebrows looked like they were stitched together in the middle.

"Dad. It was nothing. Mark's friends needed a ride somewhere. He was just trying to be nice."

"Where did they need to go?"

I paused. "They needed a ride home." That was half-true anyway.

"Beka, you have got to start working with me here. You make this so much harder on me, and yourself, when you don't obey."

"I was with someone else, Dad. What was I supposed

to do? Tell him no? He shouldn't help his friends out? I didn't know it was going to make us so late."

"I understand. But his first responsibility was to you. And to keeping his word to me."

"I called you. I let you know as soon as I could."

"And I appreciate that." Dad took a long sip of his tea. "But I don't think Mark is good for you. When you're with him . . ."

"Dad, this is not my fault. You can't do this to me."

"No, I see it as Mark's fault, and because you chose to be with him, you bear some of the responsibility."

"This is so unfair!"

"I don't know what else to do, Beka. I keep trying to give you chances, but . . ."

"But what?" I had to know.

"But I think I'm going to have to say no to you dating Mark."

I stood and ran up to my room, ignoring Dad's calls to me. I fell onto my bed and cried. I didn't know who I was madder at, Dad, Lucy, Mark, all of them. If I just got up and went downstairs and told my dad about Lucy, I could get off the hook. But should I do that? Just to get myself out of trouble?

I kicked a pillow off my bed.

God, I don't know how to get out of this mess without getting Lucy in trouble. I need to see Mark. This isn't fair. It's just not fair.

I rolled over onto my stomach and buried my face in my pillow. I wanted to go tell on Lucy. But something in me stopped me. I felt like I had done the right thing even though it backfired for me.

I stared up at my ceiling, letting my thoughts drift in every direction. I would still get to see Mark every day. Maybe it didn't matter if we couldn't officially date. There were ways around that.

And for all the right that I felt for not turning Lucy in, I felt an awful lot of wrong for the plans that were brewing inside.

You owe me big time," I told Lucy when she arrived home the next morning before church. She nodded at me glumly and went upstairs to get ready.

There had to be some rule about going to church when I was feeling so mad. Like maybe there would be a bouncer at the door who would be able to tell that things with God and me weren't too cool. But I piled into the SUV with everybody else, glaring at the back of Lucy's head and still considering turning her in.

*   *   *

"So how's school?" Nancy asked once we had settled at one of the tables in the corner of the room. Morgan and Allison had been with us until they peeled off and began chatting with some other kids. I looked at Nancy, dressed in a denim skirt and a sweater set, her blonde hair pulled back flawlessly.

"It's okay." I looked around, hoping that one of them was coming back. Nancy was being much nicer since Josh had gone away. Before that, the couple of times I got to hang out with Josh, she had seemed tense about it. I couldn't help but feel that maybe she thought I just wasn't good enough for her brother. "What about you?"

"I'm almost done, so I'm going to take some classes at the community college this year, get a jump on college."

"Are you going away to school?" No sign of Morgan, and Allison had already sat down somewhere else.

"I've been thinking about not going quite yet. I heard about this program in South Africa. I don't know. I'm praying about it. Are you going to college?"

I leaned back on the fake metal chair. The conversation reminded me of how things had been with Nancy before Josh became an issue. "The million-dollar question. Can I use a lifeline?"

Nancy laughed and rested her chin in her hand. "Don't want to talk about it?"

"It's not that." I pulled in my bottom lip and chewed on it. "Can I ask you a question?" When she nodded, I continued. "This summer. Well, you seemed like you were mad at me, and now, well, it's like everything is better. Was it Josh?"

Nancy let her head slip down until her hand was covering her forehead. After a minute she looked back up. "Was I being that obvious?"

"I don't understand."

"I'm just very protective of my big brother," she said.

My hands fell to my lap. So it *was* me.

Nancy took a deep breath. "I'm sorry. It's not you really. Josh is going to do great things for God someday, and I guess I didn't want him to get . . . distracted. You're just young. Not agewise, but in following God."

The words jabbed into me like tiny pinpricks.

"But Josh is doing great at school now, so I really didn't have anything to worry about, I guess."

Could she hear what she was saying? I didn't even know how to respond. She looked at me and smiled, but as she watched me the smile faded from her face.

"Don't take that personally. It takes time for all of us to figure out what we're doing."

I stood up. I had to get out of there.

"Beka?"

I turned and looked at her. "So as long as I'm not hanging around your brother, you'll talk to me? I thought we were friends."

"And I thought you were just using me to get to my brother."

"What?" The thought had never even crossed my mind. "I didn't even know he was your brother until after we met."

I turned and climbed over the other kids who were scattered across the carpet and ran into Dana on the way out the door.

"Beka, where are you . . ."

I never stopped; I walked straight up the stairs and went to the infant nursery, my old hideout. There it looks like I'm serving even when I'm mostly avoiding. I stepped on the gate to open it and went inside. I plastered a smile across my face. "Need some help?"

An elderly lady was in there with "June" written in shaky scrawl across a name tag.

"I love holding these wee ones. Such sweet life they hold." June stroked her wrinkled finger across the cheek of the sleeping baby in her arms. "So, what does life have in store for you?" she asked.

"Me?" I adjusted the little girl I had picked up and sat down with her in the rocking chair next to June. "I wish I knew."

"'There is a way that seems right to a man but in the end it leads to death,'" she quoted.

"Well, I don't have to worry about that, 'cause there isn't any way that seems right. Everything just seems all wrong."

"Yes?"

I looked over at the woman, rocking gently and waiting.

So I told her. All about Lucy and Mai, Mark and Josh, and now Nancy's icing on my pity-party cake.

June was silent for a while after I told her every detail.

"Boys. They'll getcha every time."

"But shouldn't it be easier than this? You like a boy; he likes you back; you go out. No big deal."

"Do you love him?" she asked.

"Which one?"

"Either one?"

Love. Was love different than a crush? Was I feeling love, or was it just the adrenaline rush of excitement that made my heart beat with a new rhythm? "I don't know. Should I know?"

"How old are you?"

"I turned seventeen this summer."

She let out a gentle laugh, careful not to wake the baby. "I met my first husband when I was your age. Mind you now, I was something to look at back then."

I smiled at that and turned the baby on my lap to my shoulder to try to get her to sleep.

"Oh, he was so full of life and easy on the eyes too. He would take me out, and we'd dance—oh, he was a fine dancer."

"What happened?"

June's face turned thoughtful. "I suppose I should have known from the beginning. We'd walk into a room, and the girls would swoon around him. Oh, he loved the attention. But it was me he chose; it was always me. Down the road he fancied the attention more than our marriage. Marriage. We were just kids. It was lovely for a time, but one day he left and found himself someone else. He swore he loved me, but it wasn't me he loved. He loved himself much more than me."

"He broke your heart?"

"I daresay I cried a river over him." June's eyes gazed ahead, surely seeing something more than the drop-tile ceiling above us. "Wasn't anything I could do, though. Shocked the town, I tell ya. Divorce was just short of complete scandal back then."

"Did you get married again?"

June's wrinkles piled up in the corners of her mouth. "Oh, yes. A fine man. He couldn't dance a lick, but he loved me. Oh, he loved me till the day he went to be with Jesus." June's eyes were a blurry red. My heart squeezed inside my chest. She turned and looked at me. "Take your time, dearie. There'll be plenty of boys for a pretty young thing like you. But don't go pickin' wildflowers on your way to the fair."

"Excuse me?"

"The fair. The place God's takin' you."

We were interrupted by Emily's mom, who came to pick her up, followed by several other parents, and I never got a chance to finish up with June. By the time every baby had been matched up with a parent, she was gone.

And I had a lot to think about.

*   *   *

"Hey, Beautiful," Mark said to me when I reached the doorway to our school. I planted my hands on my hips and shook my head. "What's wrong?" he asked.

"Thanks for returning my three phone calls this weekend."

"We went to my grandmother's."

"You have a cell phone, Mark."

Mark shook my hands loose from my hips and slipped his arms around me. "I'm not talking to you," I said.

"Yes, you are."

"No, I'm not."

"I missed you." He kissed my cheek. "When are you going to let me kiss you?"

"Well, when we're officially a couple I might be able to think about it."

Mark pulled away and grimaced.

"That's why I was trying to call you. Dad cut me off from you. I'm not allowed to see you. Fini." I drew my hand across my throat to make my point.

"'Cause you were late?"

I nodded.

Mark dropped his head back and growled, and instantly I became less concerned about being angry with him and more worried about him being angry with me. Mark brought his eyes back down to mine. "But you're still going to see me, right?"

I leaned into him and rested my head on his shoulder. "I'm not allowed."

He slipped his hand under the back of my shirt and rubbed his hand across my back. "So we'll wait it out. He'll change his mind. Right?"

I wasn't so sure.

*   *   *

Lori looked sad in second and third period, and I felt guilty for not calling her. I hadn't even found out how her date with Brian went. At lunch I gave her my attention, even though I was dying to talk to her about all my problems.

"How was Brian on Saturday?" I asked when we settled at the table with our very questionable hamburgers and fries.

She sighed. "He was the only bright spot. He went back yesterday."

"Did you talk to him about . . . you know."

She nodded. "He thinks I need to tell my mom, or somebody. He went on and on about how awful a pornography addiction could be and how he could get help from some godly men at our church and . . . well, he made a lot of arguments."

"So are you going to tell her?"

"How can I do that?"

"I don't know. But at least it's not like he's having an affair."

"Oh, that's the other thing Brian said. He said the thing Jesus said about having lust in your heart and how it's the same as adultery. So it's like an emotional affair, even though he's not physically sleeping with someone else." Lori pushed her tray away from her. "I feel sick."

"Did you want to talk to my dad?" I had nothing useful to offer her.

"Maybe. I don't know. I had a thought that maybe I should try to convince him to tell Mom what he's doing. You know, confess it."

"Do you think he would do it?"

Lori shrugged. "I never thought I'd catch him doing what he was doing, so I have no idea."

"Well, think about it. I'm sure my dad would talk to you. I'm going to see Julie today too, so I'll ask her about it, if it's okay."

"Would you? A real counselor might have a good idea." Her face brightened at the possibility.

"Sure. No problem."

It was just too bad my counseling session wasn't two hours long. I had a lot to talk about.

Okay. I guess that's it."

Julie looked at the gold watch dangling from her wrist. "Beka, you've been talking for twenty-five minutes. You have a very eventful life."

"That last part was for my friend."

Julie cocked her head, letting her short hair brush her shoulders.

"I swear. It's not my dad."

"Well, first of all, your friend really needs to get some help. I know she thinks she's protecting her family, but this thing can't be protected. It has to be exposed, or it will eat her family from the inside out."

"I think she was hoping for another suggestion."

"If she can convince her mom to come see me professionally, then I can have a family session to help her break the news. Or a pastor can do a similar thing, but it would be good to get an impartial third party, because there will be lots of heated emotions to deal with. And it will get uglier before it gets better."

I shook my head. Lori wasn't going to like hearing that.

"Now let's look at your situation. We've only got twenty minutes or so. What's weighing the heaviest on your mind?"

"Probably Mark, and the situation with my dad. And Gabby."

"That's two situations."

I had been seeing Julie since just after my hospitalization, and she had been such a big help. She was smart, stylish, and kind, and I thought she would make a perfect fit for my dad. "I was hoping my dad would ask you out." The words popped out of my mouth.

"Really?" Julie seemed caught off guard. I had never seen her flustered. She continued, "I'm flattered. Really. But I couldn't have said yes even if he did."

"Why?"

"Because I'm seeing you. It would be unethical for me to carry on a personal relationship with anyone in your family."

"Bummer. I'm going to get stuck with Gabby then, aren't I?"

"What exactly is it that bothers you so much about her?"

I dropped my head back against the couch and covered my face with my arms, letting my hands dangle by my ears. "It's not any one thing exactly. It's . . ."

I spent the rest of our time trying to sort out what I couldn't stand about Gabby. And even though I didn't reach any conclusions, I felt like what bothered me most was having a stepmother, no matter who it was.

And I didn't want to call Lori, who was probably waiting by the phone. She wasn't going to like the advice.

*   *   *

Lori got very quiet on the other end of the phone after I had explained what Julie suggested.

"Are you still there?"

"I'm here." Her voice was raspy and thin.

"The big question is, what do you think God wants you to do? Isn't that what you're always asking me?"

She didn't laugh. "Yeah." I heard her blow out her breath. "All right. I'll try talking to David, I mean Dad, first. See if he'll just confess."

"And if that doesn't fly?"

"I'll tell Mom I want counseling. She would go for it, but she'd want to know why. I really haven't kept much from her." Lori's voice broke. "She's done so much for me. How can I do this to her?"

"You didn't do anything, Lori. Nothing at all. David did it. It's his problem. His screwup. You can't blame yourself."

The crying turned soft. "Pray for me. Will you?"

"Of course I will. Call if you need anything."

I hung up the phone and dropped to my knees beside my bed and prayed. Prayed for Lori to have strength, for her dad to listen and come clean, for their family to be protected. I felt like I was really talking to Him, and He was really listening. When I finally got up, I realized thirty minutes had passed.

It was so much easier to pray for someone else than to try to figure out what God was saying to me. Julie had talked to me about that as well. How I really needed to spend time with God so I would know what He was telling me and get used to hearing His voice.

It seemed easier to do when I was sitting in her office. I pulled my Bible onto my lap and opened it. Now that I was alone with Him, I wasn't sure where to begin. Julie had mentioned a Scripture. Something about God's sheep knowing His voice. I decided to start there.

I closed my eyes. *I do want to know Your voice, God. But I'm gonna need Your help.*

I flipped to the back and looked up "sheep."

*   *   *

"You didn't call me last night," I said when I reached Lori's locker.

She flicked her eyes at me and then dropped a book onto the small shelf in her locker.

"I couldn't do it," she said.

I leaned my shoulder against the lockers and sighed.

"I tried. I really did. But he goes out of his way to avoid me. If I walk into a room, he finds a reason to leave. I couldn't even get him by himself."

"If you got him alone, would you be able to confront him?"

Lori closed her locker, and we started down the hallway. "Honestly? No. He's already mad. And if he didn't confess when I first caught him, why would he do it now? He wants me to keep quiet about it. I'm sure of it."

"But you can't."

"I know."

"Can I help?"

"Not sure yet." She gave me a half smile. "Do you think your dad would help me tell Mom?"

"I think he would. But maybe try seeing Julie. It's just such a sticky situation. Maybe a professional would be better."

She nodded, her eyes fixed. "Then I'll try to talk to Mom. She won't understand."

"One step at a time," I said.

*   *   *

My mind was focused on Lori, praying for her off and on all day, so I wasn't even thinking about myself when I walked into journalism. I probably should have been praying for myself too.

Ms. Adams waved me over after I dropped my bag by my desk. A pile of articles and flat board layouts were piled onto my desk. Every night I was taking home more newspaper work than actual homework. I didn't even look at them but went to see what Ms. Adams had for me.

Her grade book was spread out on her desk. "I'm concerned about Gretchen. This isn't really your problem, but I was wondering if you knew anything. She hasn't turned in one assignment since we started school. It's not like her. Any idea what's wrong?"

I glanced over at Gretchen's spot in the corner. She was curled up there, moving the mouse around with a glum look on her face.

"I don't know. Do you want me to say something to her?"

"No. I'm supposed to keep you two apart, but frankly she hasn't been a problem. The problem is she's doing nothing." Ms. Adams flipped the book closed, and her chair creaked as she leaned back and slid her glasses off her face.

I watched Gretchen, her hair in a short and sloppy ponytail, no makeup, and clothes that could pass for pajamas. It was like she had morphed into a completely different person. Did it happen when she was in detention, or after?

"Let me go try at least. That's part of my job, right? Managing staff?"

"If you want to." Ms. Adams put her glasses back on and reached for a pen. "These are the assignments she's missed. She's getting zeros on two assignments right now, but she can still turn these in late." She held out a piece of paper to me.

I took it and went to sit next to Gretchen. She didn't even glance my way.

"Gretchen?"

No reaction.

"You've got a couple of assignments here. You really ought to get them in."

I laid the piece of paper in front of her. She dropped

her eyes and stopped moving the mouse for a second, then focused back on the screen. "So?"

"So you don't want to fail. I thought you wanted to go to NYU. Be an actress? But you still have to finish high school."

"You sound like a guidance counselor."

"I'm just trying to help."

"Why?" Gretchen stared at the computer screen, clicking the mouse every so often.

I shrugged. Why was I trying to help her, my arch-enemy?

She's lost.

I remembered the Scripture about the sheep, and one verse popped out at me. "I lay down My life for My sheep." That's what Gretchen was. She was a lost sheep.

"Because I care about you."

Gretchen's hand stilled, and she slowly turned toward me, her eyes a blank screen.

"What?"

"Because I care about you." I paused. "God cares about you," I whispered.

Gretchen stared at me. The activity and noises in the room behind me seemed to dull as if everyone but us were under water.

"No one cares about me." She turned back to the screen, but her hand didn't move.

"Look. I know you didn't mean for what happened to happen."

I wasn't in the habit of saying things I didn't mean, so I considered my next words carefully.

"And I forgive you."

Gretchen turned to stare at me again but said nothing. She turned away.

"I forgive you." I let the words roll out again just to let myself hear them. I felt this flood of emotion that I couldn't sort out. Relief, joy, peace, everything rolled into a river that lifted me out of a dark hole I never realized I was in. I felt so light I felt like I could just float out of my chair. I almost laughed.

"I forgive you." Each time I spoke it became truer.

"I heard you," Gretchen said.

The person before me no longer felt like an enemy. She was just a girl who was very lost and very sad. She was broken.

I wished she would tell me what she was thinking. I wanted to spill out the truths I had just experienced. How forgiveness can scrub us clean. How we can care about enemies. I felt like now I could pray for Gretchen and really mean it.

Pray.

"I'll be praying for you, Gretchen."

Again, no response. I got up, but before I had even made it halfway across the room, I felt like I should have prayed for her right then and there. I had never really prayed out loud for somebody like that before, but I had heard others do it. Should I go back? I had already ended the conversation, so it would have been even weirder.

I stood in the center of the room arguing with myself. Go back. Stay. Go back. Stay.

Then Mai was standing in front of me, and my indecision was quickly replaced with a sense of dread. I should have stuck with Gretchen.

"I need you to do something for me." She folded her arms in front of her.

I lifted my eyebrows and scrunched my forehead. She had to be kidding. "Really?"

"Yeah, Lucy's coming to a party at my house this weekend, and you need to get her out of your house."

"I'm not helping Lucy do anything with you." I began to walk past her, but she reached out and snagged my elbow, standing us shoulder to shoulder.

"You might want to rethink that."

"I just want you to stay away from my sister." We were nose to nose, and she still had hold of my arm.

Her voice was just above a whisper. "Rebekah. The thing is, I bet Mark would find it more than a little upsetting to discover his girlfriend was a mental patient just last year."

I turned my head away. I should have known.

"It's Friday at ten. You know where my house is."

She let go of my arm, but my feet felt glued to the spot on the floor.

There was no way I wanted Mark to know about that.

By Friday, I had decided that Lucy going to a party wasn't that big of a deal. I wouldn't even have to lie, and I could stay and make sure she was okay.

But it nagged at me that if I didn't want people to know about the hospital, Mai probably would ask for other favors. Giving in to blackmail didn't seem like the best way to cope with the situation. Maybe I should just tell Mark myself. If it bothered him too much, then I'd know more about what kind of person he was. Trouble was, I couldn't convince myself that I cared enough about that. I didn't want to risk losing him.

*   *   *

So Friday night Lucy and I left together in the car, telling my dad it was a "sister thing." He seemed so happy we weren't fighting that he didn't ask any questions.

"You need to end this thing with Mai, Lucy. I can't keep doing this."

"Mai's my friend."

"No, she's not."

We rode the rest of the way in silence.

At least I knew I would see Mark there. I had told him about the party, and he agreed to meet me there with a big smile and a kiss.

*   *   *

The party was just beginning when we arrived. Lucy and I walked into the living room, and I spotted Mai in the kitchen. I went up to her with Lucy in tow.

"Good girl." Mai spoke as if I were a dog doing tricks. I didn't respond.

"Oh, go get a drink. Relax," Mai said. Lance came up and draped his arm around her, sticking his face where her black hair covered her neck. She smiled.

"We're not staying long. And she's not drinking." I jabbed my thumb toward Lucy.

Mai rolled her eyes and turned away. "C'mon, Lucy. Ethan's downstairs."

Lucy brushed past me, and the small group disappeared around the corner. Why was Lucy doing this? What was she trying to prove?

I would check on her in a little while, but first I

wanted to find Mark. The downstairs was filling quickly, and I made my way in a circle through the kitchen, the dining room, and into a living room. When I turned the corner I saw Mark sitting on the couch with Owen Pullman on his left and Angela Byer on his right. I swung back around the corner before he saw me and watched from behind the wall.

Angela, the same girl who had hosted the last party, crossed her long bare legs and leaned back on the couch and laughed. She swept her brown hair back away from her face and leaned toward Mark, who was giving her his complete attention. Someone bumped into me, and when I turned back to the scene in front of me, Mark had leaned closer and was whispering something to her. The soft, shy look on her face made me want to leap toward them.

Anger and fear tangled themselves up inside of me. I was mad at him, yet at the same time I had this horrible thought that I was really going to lose him. Dad wouldn't let me see him, and from the looks of it, Mark didn't want to wait around. And should he have to? Was that fair to him?

I watched Angela stand up and adjust her skirt, then fall back down on the couch, this time a little closer to Mark.

I was going to end up alone. Before Mark and Lori had come into my life, things had been so different. For months after my mom died, I barely spoke to anyone, never went out. And I had never had a boyfriend. But after this past year of being involved with people again, I just didn't want to go back to that kind of isolation. I really liked having a sort-of, unofficial boyfriend. One who gave me attention and made me feel special.

Angela laughed and slapped Mark playfully on the leg. I pressed my forehead into the wall I was hiding behind. Could I stand losing him? Or was this relationship worth fighting for? I felt anxious inside, wanting God to tell me right then and there whether I should walk away or go claim Mark as my own.

The silence inside my heart was almost unbearable. God must care about this, but He wasn't talking to me. I thought back to June talking to me in the nursery about the wildflowers. Was Mark a wildflower in my life, a pretty and nice distraction that could keep me from heading to the fair? What did God have in store for me?

The pounding music and throbbing pulse of the party swirled around me as I had my moment of crisis. Did I want Mark in my life? I did.

But did God?

I took a deep breath. *Unless You stop me, God, I'm going over there. I won't let him go unless You make me.*

Please don't make me.

I stepped from around the corner and caught Mark's eye. He grinned and stood up without a speck of guilt in his eyes.

"Hey, Beautiful. You made it." He held out his hand. "Angela and I were trying to decide whose party was better."

Angela stood up, smoothing down her skirt and adjusting her belly-baring shirt. "I'm off then. You two have fun." She didn't make eye contact with me, and a second later I was sitting in her spot, cuddled up next to Mark.

"So." I let Mark wrap his fingers around mine. "You looked pretty cozy there with Angela."

Mark laughed. "Jealous?"

"Maybe."

Mark nuzzled my neck and kissed it before he looked at me again. "There's no one but you for me."

I lifted my eyebrows. "Could have fooled me."

He took my chin in his hand and turned my face toward his. It was like every nerve ending in my body sparkled with tiny fireworks. He leaned in and kissed me, soft and full on the mouth.

I pulled away. "Are you going to get tired of waiting for me?"

"What do you mean?"

"Waiting for me to be able to go out with you. Waiting for, well, things you could probably get from other girls."

"Is that what you think of me?" Mark looked hurt.

"No. I'm just being insecure. Tell me you won't get tired of waiting."

"I won't get tired of waiting." Mark pulled me toward him until I was resting on his shoulder. I watched the party around us as I listened to the slow, steady breaths inside his chest. He rubbed my arm and kissed the top of my head.

"Is Lucy here?" he asked.

I shot up, knocking my head into his jaw.

"Ow." He rubbed his jaw.

"Sorry. I need to go check on her."

"I'll come with you."

Hand in hand we found the basement stairs and went

down. The room was packed and thick with smoke. I saw Mai and Lance kissing on a couch in a corner of the room.

I did a quick scan of the room. No Lucy.

I stood above Mai and Lance. "Where's Lucy?"

They didn't stop, and I looked at Mark, who reached over and pulled Lance's shoulder. They broke apart.

"What the . . ." Lance smiled. "Hey, man. Didn't know you were here." Mark and Lance slapped hands.

"Where is she, Mai?"

Mai gave me a condescending smile.

"I'm serious."

Mai raised an eyebrow at me, obviously unafraid of me. I looked at Lance. He shrugged. "Dude, I think she's with Ethan."

I dropped Mark's hand and bolted for the stairs. I took both flights to the second floor two at a time. I knew Mark was right behind me. I threw open every door on the second floor, to some angry protests.

I threw open the last door. Lucy sat up, wide-eyed, and Ethan jumped off the bed. His shirt was off, but she was fully clothed. "We're leaving. Now!" I yelled.

Lucy crawled off the bed, obviously embarrassed by where she had been caught.

"You stay away from her." I pointed at Ethan. At least sophomores weren't as hard to intimidate.

Lucy pushed out her bottom lip. "I like him."

"Oh, really? Well, you know what he likes about you? The fact that you came up here with him."

"I wasn't going to do anything," Lucy said.

"Sure. You were just going to talk, right? Get a clue, Luce. Do you know how stupid—"

"Yeah, and you're the poster child for purity." Lucy grabbed her bag off the dresser.

"What is that supposed to mean?" My voice dropped to a fierce whisper, and I came into the room where she was still standing by the bed.

"Look, everybody knows you're sleeping with Mark."

I felt my mouth fall open. I looked at Mark, who was still in the doorway, and then back at Lucy.

"I've never slept with him." I looked around and noticed several kids in the hallway. Mark turned and waved them away. I lowered my voice. "Go ahead and ask him if you'd like."

Lucy glanced at Mark, and Mark shoved his hands in his pockets and shook his head. "She's right. And it's not for lack of trying."

I shot him a look.

"What? I'm just kidding." He looked at Lucy. "That was a joke. Sorry."

"So, you're not . . ." Lucy's eyes dropped to the floor. She stayed that way for several minutes before she looked back up at me, her eyes glistening. "I just wanted to be popular."

"This is not the way to do it. Trust me. You're worth so much more than a quickie in some stranger's bedroom."

"I just thought since you did it, it really wasn't a big deal."

"It's a huge deal. Really huge. And you can only give it away once. Do you want it to be with someone you'll probably never see past high school, or do you want it to be with someone who you're going to spend the rest of your life with?"

Lucy bit at her top lip. "I wasn't going to do anything," she whispered.

"But you might not have stopped before something did happen. It's like skiing. Once you're headed down the hill, it's really hard to stop. Trust me."

Ethan skulked out of the room, and Mark gave him a hard look before he let him through the doorway. "And you better tell the truth about what happened up here!" I yelled after him. I turned back to Lucy.

"He was cute. And these popular girls . . . I swear it's all they talk about. I thought everybody would think I was some nerd or something if I didn't."

"You can't listen to what everybody says. You just can't. High school is four years of your life. You don't want to do stuff you're going to regret. Do you think that's what God wanted you to do? Sleep with Ethan?"

Lucy shook her head.

"Let's go. We'll finish this conversation later," I said.

Mark walked out to the car with us and kissed my cheek. "Can I see you tomorrow?" he whispered.

I shrugged. "Don't know." I looked over at Lucy slouched in the passenger seat. What kind of example was I being to her? "Call me."

"Don't tell Dad," Lucy said as soon as I closed the door.

"I'm not making any promises. You should come clean with him and get it over with."

She huffed and looked out the window.

"What's going on with you anyway? What about God?"

She didn't move for a minute, and I almost repeated the question when she finally turned toward me. "I don't know. It's just not as simple anymore. What if I'm wrong? What if I'm just talking to myself?"

"You're not."

"Everything is just so different. Paul's gone. And Gabby."

"How are you with that?"

She shrugged. "It's not really Gabby. I miss Mom. But she's not coming back. It just doesn't seem fair."

"I know. But I guess part of believing in God is believing that He knows what He's doing." I watched the yellow and white road lines slip by my car. "Even if we don't understand it."

"I haven't been talking to God lately."

"Well, then that's a good place to start. Life can get pretty confusing. And God wants to help us."

As we pulled into the driveway, I was hit with this wave of guilt. Had this been my fault? If I had been a good example for her, would she be so confused and sad? Even if it wasn't completely my fault, I was sure I didn't help things.

If I didn't have the answers, how was I going to give them to her?

Lucy told Dad on her own. She cried a lot and was way more detailed about it than I would have been. Dad's face grew redder and redder, and he spent at least twenty minutes yelling a million questions at her, never giving her a chance to respond. After he finally calmed down and grounded her indefinitely, he looked like he was caught in a fun house and couldn't get out. He kept wandering around and muttering, "I didn't think this was going to be so hard." Lucy even told him about the night I caught her at a party and admitted it was her fault I had missed curfew.

But I wasn't totally off the hook.

Dad lectured me about how I shouldn't have been at the party anyway and that I was still being irresponsible.

But he did say he was glad I helped Lucy.

"So can I see Mark?" I asked, trying to keep the eagerness out of my voice.

"Beka."

I could tell by the way he sighed that he didn't have something good to say.

I pushed back the cuticles on my fingers one at a time while he gathered his thoughts.

Please, Lord. Let him change his mind.

"Beka. I just feel like he's not who you should be with." He poked himself in the stomach. "My gut tells me that you'd be better off without him."

At least he didn't say God told him to keep me away from him.

"But."

I perked up.

"But you're seventeen. And you do need to make some decisions and be responsible for the results. I'm not going to get to follow you around college and make sure I like every guy you meet. Or date. As much as I wish I could."

"So are you saying I can go out with him?"

Dad paced the floor. "As long as you follow the rules, then, yes, I'll give you a chance to prove him and yourself to me."

"Thank you, Daddy." I threw my arms around him.

"Mind you, it's not my choice. But when I was praying for you, I felt like God told me to trust Him with you. To let Him guide you. It's the hardest thing about parenting, I think. To let you learn to follow God. 'Cause I won't always be there to step in." He stopped and faced me. "But boy, do I want to."

"Want to what?"

"Rescue you. To always be there to catch you when you fall."

"So you think I'm going to fall?"

"I don't know. I hope not. All I know is that God cares about you even more than I do. And I'm not even sure that's possible."

*　　*　　*

Our little conversation kept me up all night. By him finally saying yes, I felt like now I was even more responsible for what happened. I couldn't blame my dad; I could only blame myself. I wasn't sure I liked the new arrangement.

I called Mark as soon as I got home from church.

"I'll come get you now. We'll get some lunch."

I agreed, and he was there within thirty minutes. Dad gave me a sad smile when I asked him if I could go.

I climbed into Mark's Celica, and he leaned over and kissed me on the cheek.

"What's up? You look like you swallowed a goldfish."

"That can't look good."

"Tell me."

"Dad doesn't approve. That's all." I turned to him and watched him drive, glancing over at me every couple of minutes. He smiled and took my hand.

It was harmless, right? Having a real boyfriend. Having fun. Surely God wasn't going to deny me that. It's not like I was going to run off and get married. I wasn't making any permanent commitments or anything.

Then my thoughts flickered to Lucy, a very grounded Lucy who was back home right now. Who was watching what I did more closely than I had thought.

The sun streamed through the window, highlighting the blond in Mark's hair. God brought him to me, didn't He?

"Where are we going?"

"The beach. Mom sent some food."

I felt my spine straighten as if someone had jammed a rod down it. "I don't want to go there. Let's go out to the mountains. Remember that spot you first took me?"

"The beach is closer. And you can't stay afraid of it. Come on, baby, I want to help you with this."

Baby?

"I wasn't there for you when those creeps . . . I can't go back and fix not helping you. But I can help you with this."

I watched the trees grow shorter as we approached the inlet. Mark held on to my hand and rubbed the top of it. At least it was in the middle of the afternoon. There would be no lurking shadows. No one waiting to pounce.

I believed that in my head, but my insides didn't seem to agree. My chest felt tight, like I couldn't get a full breath. Mark drove to the very same parking lot that Josh and Paul had driven me to that night. Where the ambulance had loaded me into its belly to take me to the hospital.

The sun shone brightly, and I could hear Mark's tires crunching over the sandy pavement. He stopped the car, climbed out, and came around to my side. He opened the door and offered his hand.

We walked down to Bonfire Beach, and I looked at the spot where Liz and I had talked just before the attack. In the sunlight, the menacing images that plagued my dreams took flight. In my last dream I had been in this same spot, but all the partygoers were lit in the darkness like you would light up your face with a flashlight. They spoke unintelligible words, taunting and threatening me. I shivered the image away. No one was here. Just a beach. And a bonfire pit.

"Where did it happen?" he asked.

I pointed a finger down the beach to where the jetty hid behind the trees.

Mark pulled me in that direction as I retraced that night in my mind.

I knew I shouldn't have gone that night. Something in me told me it was pointless. If I had listened to that feeling, none of it would have happened.

I watched the tree line as we moved slowly past, and about halfway down the beach I stopped. I saw a small piece of yellow crime scene tape hanging from a slender tree just inside the wood line. I didn't think I would be able to recognize the spot, but there the tape was, announcing its memory. I turned and looked at the beach, where they had tackled me onto the sand, and then I imagined the drag marks I must have left behind as they pulled me into the woods.

Mark brushed my cheek. "I'm sorry. Maybe we should go."

I didn't even know I had started crying.

"Do you want to go?" he asked.

I shook my head and dropped his hand. I pulled the yellow tape and stared at it, wet and crumpled in my hand. I walked into the woods and easily found the clearing, the tree I had leaned against. The spot on the ground.

Mark had followed me in. "Can I do anything?"

In another dream I was here, only it didn't look the same. It was darker, and the voices I heard spinning around me were loud and angry.

I fell to the ground and touched the dirt. Even in this place God had protected me. Mark knelt down and wrapped his size around me, sheltering me. I let myself cry for a while, more in gratitude than sorrow. It could have been so much worse. They could have raped me. Killed me.

I felt Mark kissing the top of my head and running his fingers through my hair. I leaned closer, and then his lips found mine. The sweetness of him melted me down toward the ground, crowding out the fears inside.

*   *   *

By the time we walked back to the car, the pinks and oranges of the sunset had begun to tinge the edge of the horizon. I walked close to Mark, my head unable to process my thoughts. He drove me home in silence, and I stared out the window, seeing nothing.

He kissed me as I climbed out in my driveway and waved as he pulled away. I watched until his black car disappeared, my heart too crammed with emotion to think about anything except seeing him again.

*   *   *

After I had peeled off my sandy clothes and taken a hot shower, I lay across my bed and dialed Lori's number. She was the only person I could think of to call.

"Bcka, I'm so glad it's you. You won't believe . . . well, you will believe . . . but . . . can you come get me? I need to get out of here. Please." Her tense words tumbled out the second she realized it was me on the phone.

"It's almost eight."

"Please."

"Okay. I . . . uh . . . I'll be there as soon as I can." I hung up and stared at the phone for a moment before slipping into a clean pair of pants and a shirt and thumping down the stairs. I found Dad reading in the family room. That man loved his books.

"Dad. Something's up with Lori. She wants me to come get her. Can she come over?"

"What's wrong?"

I crinkled my nose. "She probably doesn't want me to tell you."

"Can I help? Is there something I can do?"

"I don't think so."

Dad looked at the clock on the VCR. "It's getting late. And you've got school in the morning."

I threw my hands up. "I know, but she sounds upset."

Dad closed his book and went over to the bookcase. "Here, take my cell. Go ahead."

"Thanks."

I got to Lori's in ten minutes. She was sitting on her front steps when I pulled into the driveway.

"I couldn't do it." She sat with her arms wrapped around her knees.

"Do what?" I sat down next to her, dropping my keys onto the cement.

"I tried." Her face looked strained, but she wasn't crying. She actually looked more scared than sad. "I told Mom I wanted to see a counselor. You know? Because Dad isn't going to tell her. And I don't want to tell her. But Dad came into the room and wanted to know why. And Mom was defending me, you know, saying that I didn't have to tell them if I didn't want to and all that, but he just kept getting angrier about it, and they were fighting, and now nobody's talking to each other, and it's my fault." She buried her face in her hands, her dark curls falling forward around her knees.

"So what do you want to do?" I asked.

"I don't know." Her voice was muffled in her hands.

The door opened behind us, and we both turned to see Megan.

"Beka. Hi. I wasn't expecting to see you." Her usual cheery voice sounded tired. She walked out and sat next to Lori.

"Are you okay? I'm sorry your dad and I were fighting. It happens sometimes."

"Not like that," Lori said.

Megan sighed.

Lori looked at me.

"Do you want me to go?" I whispered.

She shook her head and turned back to Megan. "Look. I want to tell you why I want to go to counseling."

"Sweetie, you don't have to." Megan's hand smoothed Lori's hair back. "Really. I understand."

"I need to."

Lori's face was turned to Megan, so I couldn't see her. I wanted to go. I didn't want to intrude on this, but if Lori wanted me here, I didn't want to leave her either.

"It's about you guys. Well, Dad, really."

Megan's forehead creased in worry, and fear flickered across her face. "What is it?"

Lori took a deep breath. "I caught him, four times now, on the computer looking at . . . you know, women."

Megan was silent, and her face paled under the porch light.

"You saw him?"

Lori nodded. "He told me not to tell you, but . . . everybody's telling me not to keep it a secret."

"Everybody? Who knows?"

"Well, Beka does." Megan's eyes connected to mine for a second before she flicked them away. "And she talked to her counselor about what I should do."

Megan turned and stared out into the yard, and I watched her frozen face begin to wrinkle and quiver, as she must have realized the depth of what Lori was saying.

"I'm so sorry. I'm so sorry." Lori repeated it over and over. Megan draped her arm around Lori and pulled her close. "It's not your fault," Megan said.

I felt really uncomfortable being there, and when

Megan said she needed to go inside and talk to David, I asked Lori again if I should go.

"Please don't leave. Not until I know it's going to be okay."

We followed Megan inside, but she walked right past David and went upstairs to their small office and sat at the computer. She pulled up menus and clicked furiously at the mouse as Lori and I watched.

"What's going on?"

We turned to see David in the doorway with a magazine in his hand. He looked at Lori and me and at Megan with her back to him as she worked on the computer.

"Megan?"

Lori clung to my arm and squeezed.

Megan spun around in the chair, tears streaming down her face. "How could you?"

David's shoulders dropped, and if it weren't for the fact that he was standing in the doorway, I would have run from the room.

"It's nothing, Megan." He crossed his arms across his chest, the magazine rolled up in his fist. He was clenching it enough to rip the top couple of pages.

"You're cheating on me. That's not nothing."

"What?" David exploded. "I'm not cheating. You're being ridiculous. It's nothing. It means nothing."

"Then why are you doing it?"

Lori's fingers dug into my skin, and at the same time Megan seemed to realize we were standing in the room.

"Lori, can you excuse us, please?"

David moved aside and gave Lori an unmistakable glare as we walked past him.

"And don't you dare blame her. This is on you," we heard Megan say as we went to Lori's room.

"Oh, Lori."

Lori paced around the room. "I shouldn't have told her. Did you see his face?"

I looked at my watch. It was almost ten. I flipped open the cell phone and called home, telling Dad that I couldn't get home. In answering his questions, I didn't have to go into too much detail.

Lori sat on her bed, and I pulled out the chair at her desk.

"Can I pray for you?" I said.

Lori nodded, letting a sob escape from her mouth. I moved over next to her, and we prayed. God was the only One who could help.

After a while Lori told me there was no point in me staying and convinced me she was going to be okay. I went home and told my dad everything that had happened. He shook his head and sighed a lot.

"I'm glad you could help her out. It's such a hard situation. And it's only going to get tougher for their family."

I went up to my room, almost laughing about how I never got to talk to Lori about Mark and our time in the clearing. I put my pajamas back on and curled up in my bed. I had meant to pray. It seemed like the more time I spent with Mark, the less I felt connected to God. I wanted to change that but wasn't sure how to go about it.

Especially since my prayers were mostly about Mark. Now that I could date him, I didn't feel so urgent about the matter. My mind flipped back to that afternoon.

* * *

"Mark." I pulled away from his kiss and moved his hand away from my rib cage.

"Sorry."

"It's just . . . we talked about this. Didn't we?" I said.

"You said you would reconsider when we were a couple."

"Yeah, kissing, but . . ."

Mark sat back, looking frustrated. "What is it now? I can't touch you either?"

The tone in his voice felt sharp, and I struggled to find words for the thoughts tumbling around inside.

He reached over and touched my cheek, his voice softer. "Beka. Don't you get that I love you?"

No words would come.

"I'll take it slow. I promise." He moved closer to me, his fingers fumbling with the bottom button of my blouse.

I covered his hand with mine. "I can't."

Mark's hand stilled underneath mine, and he took a long, slow breath.

"Mark. You said you didn't want to do this after what happened last time. You promised your parents. You promised me that you weren't interested in having sex right now."

Even though we were completely alone, he spoke in

hushed tones. "We don't have to have sex. There are other things . . ." His voice trailed off.

I narrowed my eyes at him, and he lifted his eyebrows at me. "All I'm saying is that we can stay completely safe and still . . . enjoy each other."

The silence between us thickened, threatening to choke me. I wasn't ready for this. What was a warm and sweet moment had again become something dark and sordid.

"It's more than just being safe or me not getting pregnant, Mark. God's real, right? You believe that?"

"Of course."

"Then He's here with us, right now. Right?"

"You're not going to do that 'What would Jesus do' thing, are you?" Mark rolled his eyes. "C'mon, Beka. We're old enough to make our own decisions." He wrapped his hand around my back and pulled me close.

"Wait." I pulled back but held onto his hand. "Listen, please." I took a breath and silently asked God for help. "It's not a 'What would Jesus do' cliché. It's about you and me. Right here. So do you believe God is here?"

"Yes, Beka." He said it the way a tired mother would speak to a toddler.

"Then, it's not just about being safe, but it's about Him being here and what He would want us to do. Look, I know it sounds silly, and it may not even be true, but my mom is with God now. If my mom could see me, then I think I would be pretty careful about what I did in front of her. Well, I don't know if my mom can see me, but I know God can."

"Beka, baby. You think too much." He shook his head

and raked his hand through his hair. "I think God likes it that we care about each other."

"Maybe. But He also makes it pretty obvious about two unmarried kids having sex."

"I'm not talking about sex!" Mark rolled back and lay flat on his back. He covered his eyes with his hand. "Why aren't you listening to me?"

"I am listening to you. But say we did . . . other things. How are we going to stop from going all the way?"

He moved his hand and looked at me. "We just would."

"I don't even trust myself to stop."

Mark watched me, but I couldn't read his expression. Was he angry? Hurt? Sad? I reached over and ran my fingers through his hair.

"I love you, Beka."

"If we love each other, then we need to protect each other. We're not anywhere near ready to get married, so we're not ready to let our bodies make some promise that we can't keep. Right?"

Mark closed his eyes, and I snuggled in next to him and rested my head on his chest. I could feel his fingers playing with my hair for a long while. I listened to the sounds of the birds and the soft crashing of the waves until he sat up and said we should go.

*   *   *

My clock glowed a bright red 12:48, and I still felt odd about the whole encounter. I didn't get the feeling Mark was happy even though I felt like I had done the right thing. When I was on the purity retreat from church back in the spring, I had felt like it never really applied to me. I never imagined that I'd have a boyfriend and be confronted with the sex issue so quickly. But one thing that was said had kept repeating itself inside of me for the past couple of days.

One of the women speakers who had spoken to just the girls asked us, "Imagine one day that you marry the man of your dreams. How are you going to feel when you have to be honest with him about your sexual history?" She had gone on to say that anything you might regret admitting to on your wedding night is something you shouldn't be doing.

Mark was fun, and he made me feel special, but I wasn't sure I could imagine marrying him. I knew that he believed in God, but I wasn't convinced that he was very interested in following God. And I felt like I was still somewhere in the middle trying to decide which way to go. I felt like there was still something missing. Or something that I hadn't figured out yet.

* * *

At school the next morning I knew something was wrong the second I arrived at my locker. A note was taped to it with my name written in big, bold letters across the front. I knew it couldn't be good.

Beka,

I'm going to give you one more chance to make sure your little secret isn't discovered. You need to resign as editor of the paper by this Friday. AND recommend me to replace you. Do this and I'll forget I even know about your episode.

It wasn't signed, but it was obvious who it was from. I closed my eyes and leaned on my locker. I felt a hand on my back and Mark's voice behind me. "Can I help?"

I folded the paper and shoved it into my bag.

"No." I smiled at him.

He leaned on the wall. He watched me, searching my face.

I lifted my eyebrows. "What? Do I have something on my face?"

He laughed. "No. Are we okay?"

"Sure. Why?"

"That whole thing yesterday."

"Yeah, I've been thinking about that."

"And?"

"Well, maybe we should only be together in public. Maybe that will help."

"If that's what you want." He sounded resigned.

I felt guilty. And I was worried that it was going to ruin the relationship. My thoughts drifted to the note in my bag. Of course, that could ruin it first.

Lori wasn't in school, and so I worried about her and about the situation with Mark more than I worried about Mai. At least I had until Friday to figure out what I was going to do.

*   *   *

After my counseling session, which basically came down to me trying to convince Julie why I wanted my hospitalization kept a secret and her trying to convince me that some secrets aren't worth keeping, I drove out to Bonfire Beach to have some time alone to think. Since Mark had taken me, I felt drawn to the place again.

But when I pulled into the parking lot, I saw Gretchen's Jeep parked in the far corner, the only car in the lot. I almost swung my car into a U-turn to find another spot, but I felt like I should stay. Was that God or just a feeling?

I parked on the opposite side of the lot and walked down to the beach, but there was no sign of Gretchen. Must have been just a feeling. I settled onto one of the logs around the bonfire pit simply because I wasn't ready to walk the tree line to the jetty by myself yet. I fell back onto the sand, leaving my legs propped up by the drift-wood, and watched the clouds and the occasional seagull float by overhead.

I loved the smell of the bay and the sand. I tried to just listen to God. Usually I felt like I needed to do all the talking, but Julie had suggested, again, that I spend more time listening.

I wanted to know two things from God: how He felt about the Mark situation and the Mai situation.

When I looked at my watch, an entire hour had passed, and I still knew nothing. Well, except maybe that I already knew what I should do about the Mai thing. If I resigned, it might delay it, but it wouldn't prevent it. Next it would be to not run for homecoming queen or go to prom, or whatever she got in her head that she wanted me to do.

I couldn't stop it. But maybe I could beat her to the punch. Confess it myself maybe. I crinkled my nose at the thought. It was the last thing I wanted to talk about with Mark. And the timing was bad. Mark wasn't really thrilled with me already. What would he think when he found out? I lifted myself up to brush off and go when I spotted someone down the beach sitting toward the bay. It could be Gretchen.

I started walking toward her high up on the beach. As I got closer, I could see her arms wrapped around her legs and that she was rocking ever so slightly back and forth. She probably wanted to be left alone. She hadn't seen me yet. I could still turn back. But as I watched her, I had that sense of how much God cared about her even if she didn't care about Him.

I walked toward her, moving to her left so that she would see me as I approached. She turned her head and shaded her eyes to see me. She looked back out to the water.

"Go away, Beka."

I almost turned back. But I felt like a kite being gently pulled toward her. I sat down close enough to talk to her.

She huffed. "You just don't listen."

"What's going on?"

She had something in her hand that she squeezed until her knuckles turned white. Her rocking became more vigorous, and her face was growing red.

"You need to go!" she said, and her voice cracked.

"Why? I'm not going to bother you."

A half-empty water bottle lay next to her covered in

sand, and her car keys glinted in the sunset next to them. I looked out at the water, wide and empty as far as I could see. Maybe I should go. Tears started streaming down her face, and her rocking had slowed.

"You're going to ruin everything. You always ruin everything."

"What? Are you waiting for someone?" I looked around. "When your friend gets here I'll leave, I promise." I felt anchored to my spot on the sand.

"So funny. I don't have any friends left, thanks to you."

So she was blaming me for what happened to her?

We sat in silence, except for her sniffles every few minutes. And I didn't even have any tissues to give her.

"Please just go away," she begged. She looked straight at me, her blue eyes rimmed with red. "At least do that for me."

I took a deep breath. Maybe I should just go. I stood up and brushed my pants off. I looked down at Gretchen, who was now motionless. I stalled just another minute.

"Gretchen? Maybe—"

Gretchen toppled over in a heap, her face in the sand.

CHAPTER 17

Becoming Beka   BECOMING BEKA

I fell on my knees next to her. "Gretchen? Gretchen?" I shook her and rolled her onto her back. Her eyes were closed, her face pale.

I leaned my face close to hers. I could feel her breath. She was breathing. I looked around me in every direction at the deserted beach.

I needed help.

"Gretchen!"

Still no response.

Maybe Gretchen had her cell phone on her. I searched her pockets and the sand around us. Nothing. I turned her gently to check underneath her, and the medicine bottle she had been clutching rolled out of her hand. I picked it up. It was empty. I didn't recognize the name of the medicine.

I leaned down again. She was still breathing, but it sounded so faint. I couldn't just leave her there to drive ten miles down the road. What if she stopped breathing? *I need help, God, right now. Please!*

Her car.

I grabbed her keys.

"I'll be right back, Gretchen. I swear I'll be right back."

I took off running, letting my sandals fly off my feet so that I could get a little more speed. I was panting by the time I reached her Jeep and fumbled with the door lock. I yanked open the door and looked in the driver's and passenger's seats. Nothing. I looked in the backseat and saw a black cloth strap. I grabbed it and Gretchen's purse slid out from underneath the seat. I unzipped it, and it took only a second to find her small silver cell phone.

I flipped it open and dialed the three numbers. I tossed the purse back in, locked the door of the Jeep, and ran back to Gretchen with the cell phone pressed to my ear.

"Nine-One-One. What is your emergency?"

"A girl. She collapsed out on Bonfire . . . I mean Breaker Beach. Near parking Lot D." I fought to get enough breath to speak and run.

"Okay. Is she breathing?"

"She was, but barely." I dropped to my knees next to Gretchen. She looked like she was dead.

"Are you there with her?"

"Yes." I panted for breath. "Is someone coming? Please?"

"Help is coming. Now I want you to check her again. Is she breathing?"

I leaned my face close and felt nothing. I grabbed her wrist and felt for a pulse. I felt it throbbing lightly under my fingertips. I leaned closer this time, turning my head to watch her chest. Did it move?

I closed my eyes and shook my head.

"Miss? Is she breathing?"

"I don't know." I tried again. This time I knew her chest moved just a little. "Yes. Yes, she's breathing."

"Did you try to wake her?"

"Yes. Yes, I tried, but she's not moving." My heart pounded in my ears.

"Calm down, miss. Do you have any idea what happened?"

"Maybe. She has an empty pill bottle." I spelled the name of the medicine to the operator and gave her the milligrams and the quantity written on the label.

"How many were in the bottle?"

"I have no idea. Please, hurry." I heard a siren whining in the distance, and I felt like a weight was lifted from me. I looked down at her, so pale and still, as the sirens grew louder and louder.

"When did she take the pills?"

"I don't know. I don't know."

I stood and looked toward the parking lot. It seemed to take forever, but finally a person in a blue jumpsuit jumped out onto the sand and scanned the beach. I lifted my arms above my head and waved. He began to sprint toward me. I sunk down onto the sand.

*   *   *

Gretchen was loaded into the back of the ambulance and whisked away, leaving me with two police officers with a lot of questions.

"Can I call my dad?" I asked.

"Sure," one of the detectives said.

"I need a phone."

The detective pointed at the cell phone in my hand.

"This isn't mine. It's Gretchen's." He held out his hand, and I put the little phone in it. "Is she going to die?"

The other detective shrugged and handed me another cell phone. "Have him meet you down at the station."

I called my dad, and as soon as I heard his voice I burst into tears. I choked out the story, and he said he would be there as soon as he could.

One of the detectives let me follow him in my car while the other one stayed behind with Gretchen's Jeep.

More yellow crime scene tape. I had to tell them everything I had touched inside her car and account for how I got her keys and a dozen other little things.

I felt like they thought I had done something to her.

I sat in a small room at the police station while they went over the story five different times with at least three different people.

My dad interrupted them. "It sounds like this girl made a suicide attempt. Why are you questioning my daughter like a suspect?"

"Sir. She's a witness. This girl, Gretchen Stanley, is in critical condition over at St. Teresa's. We're just trying to cover everything."

Dad sat back in the hard metal chair.

It took another two hours before they let us go home, and by that time, finishing my physics homework was the last thing I wanted to do.

I didn't go by the hospital, since the police told us she wouldn't be allowed any visitors. And I'm not sure she would have wanted to see me anyway.

It was after nine, but I had to at least call Lori and see if she was okay.

*   *   *

"Beka." She breathed hard. "It's a disaster. Everything's a disaster."

"What happened? I figured you'd be in school today."

"I just couldn't leave Mom. She was so sad. She threw him out, Beka."

"What? I never thought . . . That doesn't sound like her."

"I know. She's angry and really hurt. She said she needed some space and told him to find another place to stay."

"Wow, Lori. I'm so sorry."

"It's never going to be the same again, is it? This family. I thought it was the best thing that ever happened to me."

"So what happens now? Are they getting divorced?"

"I don't think so. It's just everybody's so upset right now. Mom said that she was going to the church to get counseling to figure out what to do. I just feel so guilty."

"Lori."

"I know. Mom keeps telling me it's not my fault too, but . . ."

"She's right. My dad said that it could have even gotten a lot worse. He could have started going to strip clubs or even having affairs. It's good that he got caught. I'm just sorry you had to be the one to catch him. Secrets have a way of coming out." As the words left my mouth, I laughed at the irony. "Speaking of secrets." I told Lori about Mai's note.

"You're not going to quit, are you?" she asked.

"Probably not. But it's easy to say that now. I'd just like to graduate high school with my dignity intact. Ya know?"

"She's going to tell anyway, don't you think?"

"Yeah. That's what I thought too."

*　　　*　　　*

School the next day crawled by in an eerie silence. Word had already gotten around about Gretchen, but I only heard one version of it that was remotely accurate. I couldn't stand not knowing, so I drove over to the hospital to see what was going on after dropping Lucy off. I stopped by the gift shop and bought a little balloon with Get Well across the front. I checked with the receptionist and went up to the ICU.

I saw Gretchen's mother sitting in the tiny blue and

beige waiting area just outside the enormous glass doors. She was leaning on her knees and tearing a tissue into strips. She looked up.

"Rebekah? Thank you. Thank you for finding her." She stood up and wrapped her arms around me. "If you hadn't been there . . ." Her voice trailed off into a sob.

She let go and collapsed back into the chair, balling up the soggy tissue pieces.

"How is she?" I was almost afraid to ask.

Mrs. Stanley shrugged one shoulder. "They're not sure if she'll wake up." A sob escaped from her mouth. "They just don't know anything."

I sunk into the chair next to her and laid the balloon across my lap.

"Do you want to go see her?" she asked.

"Umm, will they let me? I guess I thought . . ."

"You can come back with me."

I got up and followed her as the glass doors whooshed open and then shut behind us. We walked down to Room 8, and I could see Gretchen through the windows lying on the bed with a ventilator in her mouth.

And as I watched her there, I realized that less than a year ago, that could have been me lying there. It could have been my dad in the waiting room fighting back tears. If I had taken all those pills, what would have happened to me?

Mrs. Stanley pushed open the door, and I followed her in. She leaned over Gretchen's bed. "Baby? You've got a visitor." She reached out and smoothed Gretchen's hair out of her face, then turned to me. "You can talk to her."

I walked over next to the bed and sat on a small rolling stool. Mrs. Stanley waved and then left me there alone.

"Ummm . . . Gretchen? It's Beka." It felt weird talking to someone who was sleeping. "I guess things got kind of messed up for us. But I hope you get better. I really do." I looked around the stark room. There were only a couple of bouquets of flowers.

I sat staring at her for a while longer, then stood up and stuck the balloon into one of the bouquets. I wasn't doing any good here. I pushed open the door and left the ICU. Mrs. Stanley stood up when she saw me.

"Thanks for coming. You're the only one from school who's come." She sniffled and turned away.

I went home.

*   *   *

Every day I went by the hospital, and Gretchen's condition never changed. But I got used to talking to her. I told her all about Mai's threat and the stuff that was happening at school. I talked to her about the shows on TV she was missing and how it was probably a good thing that she couldn't eat the food from the cafeteria.

And I talked to her about God. I knew Gretchen had gotten heavily involved in witchcraft, so I told her why I chose to believe in God. I explained what Jesus did and why I decided I was going to follow Him. It was the first time I had really shared what I believed. Of course, she was unconscious, but I still talked about it. And in a weird way, talking to her about it made things seem clearer to me.

*　　*　　*

I walked into school Friday morning, braced and ready. I wasn't going to resign my editor's job. No matter what happened.

Mark was waiting at my locker. He gave me a smile. I should tell him and just get it over with. He was the only person I was worried about finding out. At least I would get the chance to explain it to him, maybe help him understand. I couldn't say anything in a hallway, but if we went out tonight or tomorrow, it would be the perfect chance.

"Hey," he said.

No "Beautiful."

"So where are we going this weekend? Since we can," I asked, pulling up on the locker handle. Mark leaned on the locker next to mine and looked around.

"I can't this weekend."

"Oh. What's up?"

"Nothing. Just something. A family thing."

"Oh." I closed the locker door and stepped up next to him. "Is something wrong?"

"No, of course not." He slid his hand behind my back and gave me a quick kiss. "Why would you think that?"

"You're just acting weird. I don't know."

"Lot on my mind," he said. "See you in theory."

And he was gone. I tossed my backpack over my shoulder and went to class, wondering if I needed to rethink my decision. If I knew why he was acting weird, it would help. Was it because of the physical stuff? Or was something else going on?

I tried to listen in my classes, all the while trying to figure out what I was going to say to Mai when she confronted me.

She was standing in the doorway of Journalism looking at her nails.

Why did high school have to be like this?

No sense in giving her any more power than she thought she had.

"Hey," I said to her, brushing past her and heading straight to my desk. When I turned she was standing right across from me.

"It's Friday," she said.

"I'm aware of that, thank you." I shuffled the papers on my desk to find Ms. Adams's "See to It" list that she left me every day.

"So how's Mark?" She crossed her hands across her stomach.

I glanced up. "Fine." The list had seven things on it. It was going to be tight getting it all done.

"Oh, well, that's good. I thought you might have broken up."

I lifted my eyebrows and shook my head, but inside I was suspicious. Why was she talking about Mark?

"So have you told Ms. Adams?" she asked.

I glanced over at Ms. Adams, who was leaning over Sabrina's desk as they looked at a paper together. I looked back at Mai.

"I'm not going to, Mai. End of story. Don't you have a column due by the end of the period?"

"Remember how fast information spreads in this school? Just look at how quick Mark found out about what you said."

Now she had my attention. "What I said? What I said about what?"

A slow smile spread across her face. "It's just a little appetizer. A sample of what I can do to you, Beka, if you don't cooperate."

I stared at her. What was she talking about? Did I even want to know?

"You only have an hour, Beka. I'd be quick about it if I were you."

I looked at the clock, but the numbers swam in front of me. *God, make this all go away. Can I please just go away?*

I buried my head in my hands. It didn't really change anything. Mai was going to tell everybody whatever she wanted. Giving her my job on top of it wasn't going to help.

I looked up and saw Liz working by herself at a desk. She had moved from Gretchen's group to Mai's, but she was still pretty sympathetic to me. I got up and pulled a chair next to her.

"Beka. Oh, hey."

"So how's your pledge going?" Liz had pledged during an assembly the last school year to not have sex and had asked me to keep her accountable. I hadn't done a very good job of it either.

"Oh." She blushed. "Well, I'm going out with Reese."

"And?" She looked away. "It's cool if you don't want to talk about it. You asked me to, remember?"

"Yeah. Thanks."

"Can you help me out, Liz? Mai insinuated that Mark was told something that I supposedly said. Do you know what she's talking about?"

Liz nodded. "Beka. I really shouldn't."

"Please? I need to know so that I can at least do some damage control."

"Mai told Todd that you were bragging to her about your college boyfriend, and how he puts Mark to shame . . . in bed, that is. Todd was supposed to tell Mark."

"What? I'm not sleeping with Mark! Do I need to tattoo it on my forehead?"

Liz held up her hand. "I'm just telling you. I didn't say it."

"Well, Mark couldn't believe that. He knows me better than that." I said it more to myself than to Liz. "Is there anything else?"

"That's all I know."

"Thanks, Liz. That means a lot." I moved away from her. It was okay, wasn't it? Mark knew me better than that. But why would he not want to see me this weekend? After all that time we waited to be able to go out. And he was distant too.

The clock ticked by, and the final bell rang. Mai looked at me from across the room. I stared back at her. The room began emptying, but she continued to stare.

As she walked by my desk she spoke almost under her breath. "It's your funeral." She slung her bag over her shoulder and bolted from the room.

It was in God's hands now.

*   *   *

I went down to the music department to find Mark, to talk to him and make sure that he knew I would never say those things. I found him in a practice room with his guitar. I watched him through the little window for a minute. He would close his eyes and strum, then stop and start again. When he opened his eyes he startled and then motioned for me to come in.

"Beka. What are you doing here?"

I leaned over and kissed him, then pulled the other metal folding chair up closer and sat down.

"What was that for?" he asked.

"You know I wouldn't say those things, right?"

His face stilled. "What?"

"Look. I didn't want to say anything about it, because I really didn't want to have to explain it all to you. All you need to know is that Mai is trying to get my job at the paper, and since I won't let her have it, she's spreading rumors again. They're just rumors."

Mark strummed at his guitar again. "I was told that

178

you have a boyfriend in college. That you're just hanging out with me because he's away. That has to be Josh, right?"

"No! Josh and I aren't anything. We're barely even friends. It's you I'm with. Not because he's away, but because I want to be here."

He looked at me from the corner of his eyes. "Do you mean that?"

"Of course I do." I picked up his guitar and put it on the floor, and I scooted as close as I could get and took his hands. "Why would you believe anything else?"

"I don't know. You just haven't been around much this week, and you don't seem to want to get more serious."

"Does serious have to be about sex? We can be serious and care about each other without getting all physical about it. Just because that's what other people do doesn't mean we have to do it that way. I like you, Mark. But I want to wait. If we really believe in God, then we'll act differently than the rest of the world."

"Where have you been this week then?"

"I've been visiting Gretchen."

"Why would you do that?"

"Because she's hurt, and I feel bad for her."

Mark snorted. "She just wants attention. Trying to kill herself. So stupid."

I felt like I had been punched in the stomach, and the room seemed to not have any air left in it. I tried to find my voice, but it came out a whisper. "How could you say that? She's in a coma."

"Beka. Why are you wasting your time with her? She obviously doesn't care about anyone else but herself."

I stood up. "You know, Mark, you use the name 'God' every once in a while, but you don't seem to care much about what He says, do you?"

"What?"

"I haven't read much of the Bible, but even with the little bit I have read I know that half of what you're saying is just wrong. It's not about the sex, or Josh, or some stupid rumors, Mark. I want to be with a guy who at least lives up to what he says he believes."

I turned and walked out of the room and took giant steps down the hallway. I didn't look back, but part of me hoped he would come running and apologize. That he would promise to change. But I reached the journalism room before I realized that Mark was nowhere. And I was very much alone.

*   *   *

I locked up the journalism room and drove to the hospital to sit with Gretchen awhile. Even though she never spoke, blinked, or moved, I felt like I was visiting a friend. When I was done, I went home and called Lori. There was no sense in staying home on a perfectly good Friday night just because of Mark.

*   *   *

"Thank you, Beka. I needed to get out of the house." Lori leaned back in the passenger seat and sighed.

"What's been happening?"

"Dad's back, but he's in the guest room right now, and we have a counseling session tomorrow morning. I'm scared though. He looks at me like I betrayed him. He'll never trust me again."

"It'll probably just take some time."

"That's not the worst of it though. The whole church knows about it. It just feels like everybody's pointing and staring when we go, especially since Dad won't go."

"I'm sorry."

"I know. Look, let's not talk about anything bad tonight. Let's just have fun, 'kay?"

I smiled. Lori was just what I needed.

We went to two different movies and laughed till our sides hurt. We decided comedy was a much smarter choice for us. By the time we got to The Fire Escape it was almost eleven. We ordered some milkshakes and sat at a table, repeating our favorite parts of the movies.

Then I saw Mai walk in with a large group. The coffee/dessert bar was set up with windows all along the front and a section of tables along the windows to the right of the counter. The patio doors were wide open, and more kids mingled out there. We were at a back corner table, but we still had a view of the entire place. Mai spotted me easily.

"There's the woman of the hour!" she yelled. Even over the music everybody heard. The place was packed with people both inside and on the patio. She sounded a little drunk, which wouldn't have surprised me. Lance had his arm around her, but she threw it off and pointed at me, then tripped toward me.

"Yep. Did you all know?" She turned and looked behind her at her friends. "What little Beka's secret is?" Mai grinned and then laughed.

Lori grabbed my forearm and squeezed.

"Well." She huffed the word out and then made circles with her finger near her head. "Beka's crazy. Not just your everyday crazy either. She was shipped off to the loony bin because she tried to kill herself. Poor little Beka."

I could feel the stares as people listened to Mai and looked at me as if they could tell by looking if what she was saying was true.

"Anybody have a straitjacket ready in case she goes nuts?" Mai laughed loudly and slapped her hand on our table. She looked me in the eye. "People like her shouldn't be out on the streets. You know what I mean?" Mai stood up and stumbled back to her friends at the counter.

"Should we just go?" Lori asked.

I shook my head. The damage was already done. "I don't want to cause another scene."

"Are you okay?" she asked.

"I will be. At least she doesn't have anything to hang over me anymore. Right?"

I scanned the restaurant, noticing that some people seemed to be whispering and looking at me out of the corners of their eyes. I turned in my chair and looked out onto the patio to see who else had heard Mai's announcement. I recognized a few kids from school.

Then a whole group from the patio stood and came through the door, and sitting by himself at a table stirring a drink was Mark.

And he was looking right at me.

"Oh, no." I turned back and buried my face in my arm on the table. "Mark's here."

"Oh, Beka." I could feel her patting my arm. "He's coming this way," she whispered.

"Tell him to go away," I said.

"Hi, Mark."

"Hi, Lori."

I could just imagine the looks on their faces.

"I don't think she wants to talk," Lori said.

I could hear a chair being dragged nearby, but I wasn't about to lift my head. After a minute I asked, "Is he gone?"

"Nope. He's sitting with us," Lori said.

If I sat up my face was going to be red from where I had been pressing it into my arm. There was no graceful way out of this.

I lifted my head slowly and brushed the hair out of my face to see Mark drinking from a sweaty glass. He put his drink down and leaned forward.

"So. Is it true?"

CHAPTER 15

Becoming Beka   Becoming Beka

Yes. It's true."

"You must think I'm a total jerk," he said.

"The thought did cross my mind."

"Will you tell me about it? Your version. Not hers."
He pointed a thumb behind him where Mai's loud laugh
could still be heard.

I rolled my eyes, and Lori looked at me with a mix-
ture of sympathy and sadness.

"Fine. I did stay at the psych hospital just before
Christmas last year. I thought about taking some pills,
and even though I didn't actually take them, my dad
freaked out, and they admitted me."

Mark's expression didn't change. Did I need to tell him the whole story, or could he just fill in the gaps?

"Anyway, I had a lot going on, and I wouldn't talk to anybody to get help, so I ended up feeling like I had no other way out. It wasn't true, but that's the way I felt. So that's why I've been visiting Gretchen. I know how she felt."

"But you lost your mom, Beka. Gretchen caused her own chaos."

"It doesn't matter. It's scary to feel like you're all alone. You said it yourself today. That people who do that are just looking for attention and that it's stupid. That makes it even harder to ask for help."

Mark closed his eyes for a long second and took a deep breath. He opened his eyes. "Sorry."

"And while I'm admitting to things, I'm in counseling too. I really like going; it helps me sort stuff out. So there." If he was going to dump me, he might as well have all the information.

I waited for as long as I could stand. "Say something, please."

"I don't know what to say."

"Well, we've gotta go anyway." I stood up, and Lori jumped out of her chair. "See you on Monday." We walked out, and once again my body tensed, hoping he would come after us. But we reached the car and climbed in, and he still hadn't followed us. The laughter we had enjoyed earlier had completely vanished.

I dropped Lori off and drove home in a cloud. Was Mark really that shallow? I didn't know what to think of his reaction—or non-reaction. The one thing I was sure of was that I wasn't too eager to go to school.

*　　*　　*

We were already in the church parking lot on Sunday morning before I realized that Nancy would probably be there. I knew I should probably say something, but I honestly felt like a third-class passenger on the Titanic. I was always going to be behind in the spiritual department and not good enough to hang out with the first-class passengers.

As soon as I turned the corner I saw her standing outside the classroom door. I drew in my breath and held it for a moment. She was tapping her shoe on the wall behind her, but when she saw me she pushed off the wall and walked toward me.

"I should have called you, but I wanted to do this in person. I was wrong. Totally wrong to say that to you. It's more about Josh than you. And I shouldn't have acted like you weren't good enough or suggest that he would be better off with someone else. It just wasn't fair or right, and I'm so sorry. Really, really sorry." Her eyes widened as she watched for my reaction.

"I just feel like you're always going to see me way behind you, and him, trying to catch up."

She cringed. "And that's not true at all. Beka, I don't have any more of God inside me than you do. Trust me. And things like this remind me that I have so much to learn, and no matter how old I get I'll still have to learn stuff. My pride showed up and attacked you. I'm really sorry."

Until that moment I hadn't realized how much her comment hurt me inside, but the emotion welled up inside me and threatened to escape. How I felt about Nancy was the same way I felt about Josh. Too good for me to be around. That, combined with Josh being away, made me feel like Josh was a hopeless fantasy.

I loved the way Josh treated me so carefully. I would never have to argue with him about anything physical, because he wouldn't even try. Mark sometimes made me feel like that was the only thing that mattered anymore. Mark made me feel special when I was with him, but with Josh I felt like I was worth something whether he was with me or not.

And until that moment I hadn't realized there was a difference.

"It's okay. I forgive you. I can certainly understand."

"But you shouldn't, because it was my own stupid sin. Not yours. I don't want to mess up things with you and Josh."

"There isn't anything between me and Josh. We're just friends."

Nancy lowered her chin and lifted her eyebrows.

"No, really. He told me in Haiti that there was 'no obligation.' I figured he meant that so he could see other people."

"Maybe. But it's you he asks about when he calls."

"Really?" My heart swelled just a little. "He's just so far away. Even being friends is kind of pointless."

Nancy smiled. "We have a way of making plans and making decisions, but when it comes right down to it, God knows what's best for us. He'll get you to where you need to be."

And where was that?

Nancy hugged me. "Are we okay?" she asked.

"Sure. Tell him I said hello."

"Absolutely."

*　　*　　*

Gabby came over for lunch after church. I did my best to be pleasant, but it was like there was a steel wall I couldn't break through with her. Everything she did annoyed me. And the way my dad looked at her annoyed me. And when Anna smiled at her it annoyed me.

I picked at my food and pushed it around on my plate until it was cold and gross, only half-listening to the conversation around me.

"So what do you think, Beka?"

"Huh?" I looked up.

"Didn't you hear any of that?" Dad asked.

"Sorry."

"I thought maybe we could do a little shopping, just you and me. Maybe get some dinner." Gabby smiled and took a drink from her glass. It was so quiet I could hear the ice shift and pop.

"I can pick out my own clothes."

"That's not the point, Beka," Dad said, his tone firm.

"Fine. Whatever."

"Can I go too?" Anna asked.

I was about to say yes when Dad said, "Not today, Miracle."

She pouted but didn't say anything.

"Well, I need to go turn out the horses, but I can be back in an hour. I'll come pick you up. Okay?"

I shrugged.

She left, and I started clearing the table to do the dishes.

"Be nice," Dad said as he brought me a couple of bowls from the table.

"I'll try." But even as I said it I wanted to go crawl in my bed and not come out. An entire afternoon and dinner with Gabby. I wanted to sit in my room and plot my reaction to school the next morning, stressing over what might happen. I didn't want to spend it making nice with Gabby.

*   *   *

She was right on time. I went out to meet her and climbed into her truck. Figures a horsewoman would drive a truck. I buckled my seat belt and folded my hands in my lap.

The awkward silence had already begun.

I thought back to my little bowling alley revelation. I shouldn't be mean to her. I knew it, but everything in me wanted to scare her away from my family.

I wanted my mom back.

More than anything else, that's what I really wanted.

I turned and looked out the window so she wouldn't see the tears that I was powerless to stop. I missed Mom. Nobody would ever look at me the way she used to. Even when she didn't understand me. Even when I was keeping secrets, she looked at me like I was the most important, amazing person in the world. No matter what, she loved me completely.

The overwhelming sadness moved aside as anger flared up. Why did she have to go away? She should be here. She should be here for me. It wasn't fair that I was stuck here trying to deal with life while she was enjoying paradise.

Then as quickly as it lit, the burning subsided.

It wasn't her fault. She didn't choose to go. She would never have chosen to leave us behind. I let the tears drip onto my arm and down into my lap.

It wasn't her fault, was it, God? It happened. And I'm really glad she's in a better place. I'm so glad she's with You. Forgive me, Lord. Please? I've been so upset and angry with You. With her. Mom, I know you didn't want to go away. I forgive you . . . for leaving me here. I'm sorry I've been such a brat. Lord, please help me love again.

As the sentence formed in my head, a fresh set of tears escaped.

I needed to know how to love again.

I didn't really love anybody anymore. I couldn't even say the words anymore. I was scared of losing everyone else. If God could take my mom away, then nothing seemed safe anymore. That was no way to live. That wasn't the way God wanted me to live.

I need to know how You love me, Lord. Show me. Show me Your love so I can love again. Help me let go.

The tears slowed. Gabby hadn't said a word, but as we pulled into the mall parking lot, she shifted the car into park and turned the engine off. I turned and looked at her, and she looked back, her eyes filled with hope and sadness.

"Are you okay?"

I nodded and sniffed. Gabby dug around in her purse for a pack of tissues, and she handed me two. I unfolded them and blew my nose and wiped my eyes. I flipped down the visor to make sure my mascara wasn't smeared across my face. I wiped under my eyes and then flipped it back up and leaned back on the seat.

"I owe you an apology."

She held up her hand. "Beka. It's okay. I understand how you must—"

"No, really. Let me say this. It's not you I've been mad at; it was the whole thing. My mom dying. God taking her away. I've been shutting everybody out so I won't get hurt again. And I've been awful to you. You going away isn't going to bring my mom back or make anything better." I stopped and thought for a moment. "You're good for my dad. You made him smile again."

A tear dripped down Gabby's cheek.

"I still need to figure out how to unwrap myself from all of it, so I know I'm not fixed yet, but I'll try. I really will."

"Can I help somehow?"

I shook my head. "Just give me some time."

"You've got it, kiddo." She laughed and then covered her mouth. "Sorry. I laugh when I get nervous."

I smiled. "That's okay. I really am sorry."

"It's all good. So, should we do some shopping?"

"Sure. I've had my eye on a cropped jacket."

*　　　*　　　*

We spent the entire afternoon walking around the mall and talking. She was a pretty interesting person, and I could hardly believe that I actually wanted to know more about her. It was like God had dismantled the steel wall inside and let me care again. I still felt like I was learning to swim, but I wasn't so scared anymore.

I even told her about Mark and Josh. Which was a huge step for me.

A good step.

My stomach churned all the way to school. Refusing breakfast may have been a mistake, since the hunger pains made me even more jittery. I walked into school and stood in front of my locker. A thick piece of masking tape was taped on my locker, and the letters P-S-Y-C-H-O were scrawled across it.

How stupid. I ripped it off, but the tape shredded, and I had to pull it off piece by piece.

Lori came over and started helping.

"What did it say?"

"Psycho."

I pulled off a long piece and balled it up.

And that was just the beginning.

On my way to first period, at least three people called me psycho, and I found another note on my locker before lunch. A couple of kids made comments like "Oh, better not be mean to her; she might lose it," and I heard a lot of "poor little Beka" comments. But some kids were just plain cruel, telling me I should have tried harder or suggesting other methods.

I tried to ignore them all.

But the worst part really wasn't what they said. It was the way they looked at me. Maybe I was just being completely paranoid, but I felt like everybody was staring and talking about me. Conversations seemed to stop whenever I walked by, and people whispered about how I was the "other girl" who tried to kill herself. By the time I got to journalism class I felt like screaming. It was like swimming in a fishbowl all day, with sharks outside of it.

Ms. Adams called me over as soon as I walked in the room.

"Beka. I need to talk to you about something. Pull your chair over."

I went and dropped my bag and grabbed my chair, scared that I was going to get fired. Did she think I was unstable or something?

"Here it is. The administration wants to hold an assembly on Wednesday because of what happened with Gretchen. They don't want any copycats. The assembly is not about Gretchen; it's more about . . ." She picked up a paper and read off of it. "How to get help if you need it. Who you can talk to. How you know a friend's in trouble, etc."

"Okay."

"They want the paper to run some of the information from the assembly this Friday so the students have it to take with them. Can you divvy out some assignments to get that covered?"

I nodded.

"Here's the list. And there's one more thing. They asked me if I knew of any students who might be willing to, well, give a student's perspective."

"On what? On Gretchen?"

"No. About suicide. You could research it and talk about it as a peer. Sometimes that works better if they hear it from someone their own age."

"*I* could?"

"I thought as the senior editor you would be in a great position to report on it."

"What about the class president? Doesn't that make more sense?"

"That's just a popularity contest. Who knows what might come out of her mouth when she got up there? Would you think about it today? And let me know at the end of class?"

"Sure." I went back to my desk and sat down with the memo from the office. I didn't know what to do. I didn't want to say no without a decent reason. Ms. Adams had taken a chance on me being editor, and I owed her for that. But speak? In front of the whole school? I felt nauseous just thinking about it.

But the more I thought about it, the more it seemed like a God thing. I had heard Nancy use that phrase to describe something only God would have come up with.

It would give me the chance to set the record straight. Everybody was already talking about me anyway.

It could even help someone. Our school was full of "fringers," those kids who hung on the sidelines of school life, always on the outside looking in. Then again, anybody could feel hopeless enough to consider ending it all. Even I did.

There was the question of whether or not I could get my mouth to work once I got up there. Courage. It was hard for me to step out and try something new. But the next year would be full of new things: applying to college, moving away from home. I couldn't just sit back hoping that nothing would ever change and hide from it. In this case, I could even use the change to my own advantage. And what Mai meant to destroy me, I would turn into something good. Or at least God could.

After the bell I told Ms. Adams I would do it, and she gave me a hug. Now all I had to do was prepare for it.

*   *   *

The next two days were a blur. I spent every free moment in the library or in the newspaper room researching what I was going to say. I only had five minutes, so I didn't need a lot of material, but I wanted the right material. Only Lori talked to me at school, but I barely noticed anyway. By Wednesday I was ready to go. And scared to death.

Lori stood with me backstage during the program to help me. She prayed for me, and I tried not to hyperventilate with the deep breaths I was taking trying to slow my heart rate. My entire school was out there. When I had played Annie in the musical, I was dressed up as someone else. This time it was just me.

I closed my eyes. *Lord, I need strength. I can't do this by myself. I'll mess it up. But I think You want me here. So help me say what You want me to say.*

"And now, I'd like to introduce Rebekah Madison, a senior and the student editor of *The Bragg About.*"

I looked down at my notes. I would start with the statistics. Lori patted me on the back, and I walked out to some very unenthusiastic applause.

I stood behind the podium and adjusted the microphone.

Take your time.

I looked out at Bragg County High School. Mai was out there somewhere. And Mark.

"I wanted to die once." The words appeared in my mouth as if someone else had said them. And they definitely weren't in my notes.

"We all feel alone sometimes. Isolated. Cut off. Sometimes things happen that make us feel hopeless or depressed. We may even feel like our lives are over. But they are only over if we let them be over.

"My mother died early last year. Many of you know that. I didn't want to talk to anybody. Who else could understand what I was feeling? And yes, I began to think that if I died, then my pain would end. I spent some time in a hospital and in counseling, and I learned a few things along the way that I'd like to share with you.

"The first thing is that there are people who can help. Mr. Erney just talked to you about all the places you can get help if you need it. And if you're thinking of dying, then you do need help. Once we've crawled into that dark pit, it can be hard to find our way out unless someone comes along to shine a light for us. And these people not only can help; they want to help."

I gave some examples of people who they might consider talking to and explained how asking for help may be hard, but said that once they did, the hard part was over.

"The second thing is that life really is worth living. Even when it stinks."

A small chuckle rippled through the audience.

"Life isn't easy or fair. And high school can be tough. But this part of our life will end, and we'll go on to a new part, a new adventure. And we'll miss out on it if we give up on life too soon."

I gave some examples of the dreams and plans that I knew many of them had. I pointed out that it takes time and courage to reach our goals, but that we have to keep pressing on even when it's hard.

"And that brings me to my last point. Tomorrow is a new day. When things happen that we don't want or expect, they bring with them the opportunity for something new. So your boyfriend dumped you. You have the chance to find a nicer one. So you didn't get into the college you wanted. Maybe the one you did get into will be better. So high school is hard. College can be better. Even when someone dies, our lives are never empty of people willing to care about us. And love us. But we have to give life a chance. You're worth it. Thank you."

It was silent just long enough for a sweat to break out on my forehead. Was it that bad? Then the room broke into a roaring applause that I could hardly believe. Mr. Erney tapped on the microphone to get everybody to settle down, and I hurried offstage.

Lori gave me a hug. "That was awesome."

"What did I say?"

Lori leaned back. "Duh? It's right here." She picked up my notes and scanned each of the three pages. "You didn't say any of this."

"I know."

"Oh, well. It was awesome. Maybe you have a future in public speaking."

I grabbed my notes back. "But I didn't back up what I said. I had all these great statistics. Look, see my list?" I pointed at the page.

Lori laughed. "I don't think anybody cares. You said what they needed to hear. Let the rest go."

Everywhere I went for the rest of the day kids were walking up to me and thanking me for what I said. It was a total turnaround from the first part of the week. A guy named Daniel, whom I had hardly ever heard speak before, even asked me out. I told him I couldn't, but it was sweet of him.

It made me think of Mark, of course.

During journalism class I asked to be excused, and I went to go find Mark in the music wing. I found him in his regular rehearsal room with his guitar on his lap.

"Hey, Beautiful."

So we were back to Beautiful?

I went in and sat down across from him.

"We need to talk."

Mark rolled his eyes. "What this time?"

"I just need to know where we stand. What are we?" I watched him and searched his face, but I couldn't read him. He still seemed so distant.

"I thought you were with someone else."

"I told you that wasn't true, Mark. You don't believe me?"

He shrugged and picked at his guitar strings. "I just won't be made a fool of."

Tears sprang into my eyes. I really could lose him.

"Mark, I told you. Mai made all that up. She threatened to tell everybody about the hospital. I just didn't want everybody knowing."

"Beka. I just think you want some perfect Christian guy. That's not me. I believe. I really do. But I'm just not sure what that looks like for me yet."

"I thought you wanted to get things right with God. You told me that."

"I do. But I want to enjoy my life too. You make me feel like I need to always be thinking about what God thinks. I don't know what He thinks. You're just so serious about it." He strummed at the guitar, and I stared at him.

"So that's it? After all your talking and promises, that's it?"

"We can still go out, have some fun, but let's not get so serious."

"Can you just spell it out for me so I'm perfectly clear? So, you want to date?"

"Sure."

"But not just me?"

"Well, I just think we need to keep things light, you know?"

"You're the one that wanted to be more serious. I don't get it. What changed?" I fought to keep the tears out of my voice and off my face. "You said you loved me."

"I do. But I guess I'm not enough for you."

"Mark! Why don't you believe me? Nothing is going on with Josh. He lives three thousand miles away." I stood up but had nowhere to pace in the small room. "I have nothing else to say. What's the point anyway? You don't believe me."

I walked out before the tears began rolling down my checks. That was it? That was how it was going to end? What had messed everything up so badly?

I found a bathroom and slid into one of the corners and cried. Fortunately it was an out-of-the-way bathroom, so no one came in. I hadn't wanted to lose Mark. Even though I wasn't sure about the whole thing, I didn't want him to dump me.

I drove home instead of going to the hospital. I didn't think I was finished crying yet. I brought in the mail, and in it I found a letter from Josh. I sat right down on the porch and opened the envelope. His timing was perfect.

Dear Beka,

I hope all is well with your soul these days. I still love it here in Seattle even though it only ever seems to rain. I was reading my World Cultures textbook today and in flipping through I saw a picture of Haiti. When we were there I looked out the window of the clinic one day and saw you

*surrounded by these shining dark faces as you strummed on
that old guitar. You had a huge smile on your face and the
kids kept pushing closer just to get near you. There must have
been thirty of them surrounding you as you sang to them.
That's the picture I have of you inside of me.*

*I'm not sure I should tell you this, but I went out on a
date the other night.*

I held the paper away from me as if it were a rattle-
snake. No. Please, no. This isn't fair. I cried again. Somehow it was easier to cry when I had already been sobbing
that day. It was one of those moments when I just wanted someone to hold me and tell me that everything was
going to be okay.

I opened the paper back up. Not reading it wasn't
going to make it go away. I found my place.

Her name was Dynah and she was really nice.

I really didn't want to hear this. I knew this pen pal
thing wasn't going to work.

*I asked her out because it seemed like the thing to do. It's
different out here. I've met a lot of students that are already
married and living off campus. But the whole time I was
with her, I couldn't stop thinking about you.*

I gasped and read the sentence again.

*I couldn't stop thinking about you. Not just that image of
you in Haiti, but you at church, you in that beautiful green*

dress. You smiling at me. Maybe it's not fair to tell you all this because I'm so far away. But I wanted you to know that someone is thinking of you. Right now.

Josh

P.S. I won't be going out with Dynah again.

I stared at the paper and read it two more times. What did that mean? I flipped it over but there was no more writing. There didn't seem to be some secret coded message. He thinks about me. He's not going out with this girl again. What did it mean?

Gretchen woke up. Apparently Mrs. Stanley called my dad at the bank, begging him to let me know. So he called over to the school, and I left for the hospital after the final bell. Talking to Gretchen while she was asleep was one thing. Gretchen awake was a whole other story.

I parked the car and was directed to her new room on the fourth floor.

"Well, don't just stand there," she said when I stepped into the open doorway and hovered there.

I came in and sat down in a chair. What was I supposed to say?

"Mom said you came by."

"Yeah."

"I should be mad at you."

"What? For saving your life? Again?"

Gretchen leaned back on her bed, the top of which was positioned almost upright.

We looked at each other. Even after the coma, she looked better than she had in the days before she tried to kill herself.

"They're going to put me in the psych hospital. Probably tomorrow."

"I figured."

Gretchen pulled at her hair. "Is it bad? I mean, they don't, like, tie you down on the bed or anything, do they?"

I laughed. "No. You'll do lots of talking about 'your issues' though."

"My issues?" She rolled her eyes and snorted. "Great. I'll be in there the rest of my life."

"Nah. It's the adolescent wing. When you turn eighteen they'd move you to the adult side."

She narrowed her eyes for a moment, then laughed. I joined in, but the moment dissipated quickly.

"So, did you, like, pray for me?"

I shrugged. "Yeah, I did."

Another silence filled the room, so I stood up to leave. "I better get going. I'm glad you're better."

"Okay."

I was in the hallway when she called my name. I turned back to her.

"Thanks, Madison."

"Sure."

*　　*　　*

The weeks began to fly by as I got buried in my senior year classwork, and since Mark was just a tormenting presence at school, I spent my weekends visiting colleges with my dad. He made me promise I would apply to five schools, and since I didn't have any good ideas on what to study, I felt like I was starting from scratch. Big school or small school? Urban or suburban? Brick or modern? Christian or nonreligious? The choices seemed positively endless, and the more I thought about it, the more my head hurt.

I had sent away for a brochure to Seattle Pacific, and I flipped through it. It did look great, but I knew my dad wasn't willing to let me go that far away. I heard kids talking at school about their first choice and safety schools, but I wasn't really excited about college. It just seemed like the next logical step.

I enjoyed the college visits, and we got to spend a weekend at Paul's school, which was great. He even took me to two of his classes.

We had lunch, just the two of us, in the campus food court.

"So Dad's dragging you around, huh?"

"Yeah. It's good though. There's just too much to choose from." I took a bite of my salad.

"You'd like it here. It's kind of low-key, not too big. I like it."

"But how did you know? That you should come here?"

Paul shrugged with one shoulder. "It just seemed right. Inside."

"When though? When you first looked at it?"

"I don't know. What's with the third degree?"

I put my fork down and leaned back in the chair. "I just don't know what I'm supposed to do. And there's all this pressure!"

Paul laughed.

"Do you see me laughing?"

That just made him laugh harder. "Beka. You'll figure it all out. You don't need to stress out about it. We'll stop talking about it if it's going to freak you out. How're things at home?"

"Gabby and Dad are dating."

"I heard. You okay with that?"

"Are you?"

"Sure. Dad shouldn't have to spend the rest of his life alone. Are Lucy and Anna okay with it?"

"The dating part, I guess. Do you think they'll get married?" I pulled at the pocket on my pants.

"I would guess that's where it's heading. Right?"

We finished our lunch and met Dad so that we could drive home. It was hard leaving Paul. It felt different with him being almost five hours away and too busy to come home very often. I had actually hoped he would have some sort of grand insight as to where I was supposed to go to college, so I left feeling deflated and tired.

*   *   *

Mark pretty much avoided me at school except in music theory, where he acted like another teacher instead of what he once was. I stared at him sorting through papers on Thompson's desk as Thompson went on and on about chord progressions. I still couldn't figure out where things went so wrong. Or why I wanted him back so bad.

Josh was writing at least once a week, making it seem like he really cared about me, but the Seattle thing always kept me from getting too excited about it. He was coming home for Christmas and wanted to see me, but what good would that do? He'd leave again, and it would be another six months until summer came. And then next fall I'd be busy at my own college. Unless, of course, I applied to Seattle Pacific.

Mark ran his hand through his hair and chewed on his top lip. What could I do? I had even heard he was dating Angela. Which would totally figure.

Thompson let us have "project time" each day, which was just the last ten minutes of every class that we could use for our semester project. When he let us go, I went over and sat with Janne, one of our foreign exchange students. He was helping me with the song I was trying to write.

I handed him the piece of paper with the changes I had made, and he stared at it, nodding at it. "This is good," he said with his thick accent. "You changed the bridge. I think this will work better."

He picked up his guitar. "Close your eyes and listen."

He played and sang the first verse. I opened my eyes.

"You hear it. We need to work on this transition. Any ideas?"

We worked on it for the rest of the period, and he gave me what to work on for the next day. It was coming along, but it was so much harder than I expected. The song came from inside me, felt like part of my soul, but constructing the song was more like trying to build a house. Each part had to be built just right so that it would all hold together.

I had no idea it would be so hard . . . and so much fun.

*   *   *

Life had settled into a kind of pattern, but right after Thanksgiving, it all started to change again. At first I had no idea it was all going to lead to such a life-changing decision. I'm almost glad I didn't know.

Dad had given me until December 22, our last day of school before winter break, to finish all of my college applications. He said he didn't want me grumpy over the holidays, so even though the deadlines were mostly in January, I was stuck getting them done early.

And they weren't much fun to do. All the demographic info was pretty easy, but the essays were hard. I just wasn't sure what to say, and I kept thinking, *If I say this, how is it going to make me sound to them?* I typed and erased every line and stared at the computer, wishing it would just appear on the screen in front of me.

Lori was supposed to come over to spend the night, so I didn't have much time. I was determined to finish at least one of the essays.

A knock came at the door.

"What?" How was I supposed to finish if people kept bothering me?

"It's me." Lori pushed open the door. I could tell she had been crying.

"What happened?" I asked.

She dropped her bag on the floor and flopped onto my bed. I went and sat up at the top of the bed. It was always best to give Lori a chance to talk.

"It's all such a mess." She propped up on one elbow and looked at me. "It would have been better if I hadn't ever come to their family. Really."

"Don't say that. I thought things were going good."

"I thought so too. They were in counseling. He was living at home. I mean, I knew he was still upset by the whole thing, but while we were at my grandmother's for Thanksgiving, he just, I don't know, exploded or something."

"Go on."

"He just thinks it's all ridiculous and that everyone is overreacting about it. They put these guards on the computer at home and in his office—and he agreed to it. And he was supposed to meet with a pastor every week to get support and help make sure he was staying away from it, you know? But I guess he didn't think he deserved to have all these people prying into his life. He's just so mad. And he threatened to leave if everybody kept bothering him about it."

"Leave your grandmother's?"

"No, leave Mom."

I closed my eyes for a minute. I didn't know what to say.

"If I had never come, then none of this would have

happened." She laid her head on her elbow and then rolled onto her back.

"Lori. Quit saying that. David would still have done it. You being there didn't make him look at those pictures. It's his fault, not yours."

"That's not the way it feels."

"There's sometimes a difference between what is true and what we feel. You've got to choose to believe what's true. It's not your fault."

"What if he does leave though? I know it's totally selfish to say this, but what about college and all of that? I don't know if Mom can still send me if he walks out."

"He'd still have to help out. It's just going to take some time."

My phone rang.

"Do you want me to let the voice mail get it?" I asked.

"Go ahead."

The caller ID said Stanley. Now that was weird.

"Hello?"

"Beka? It's Gretchen."

"Oh. Hi." I covered the receiver with my hand and mouthed, "It's Gretchen" to Lori. Her eyes widened and she sat up.

"I was wondering if you could meet me at The Rock Garden tonight."

"Well, I have Lori over tonight."

"She can come too. Actually, that would be good."

"Oh. Okay." We agreed on a time to meet, and I clicked the phone off.

"What?" Lori asked.

"She wants us to meet her."

"Us? So we're going?"

"Why not?"

We drove out to the little diner and found a booth. There was no sign of Gretchen.

"So do you hear from her regularly?" Lori asked.

"No. Not really at all since she woke up from the coma. She transferred to Lakeland High. It would have been hard to come back to Bragg County."

"I guess."

We ordered drinks, and a few minutes later Lori whispered, "Here she comes."

Thanks for coming," Gretchen said as she slid into the booth. The waitress came over, Gretchen ordered a soda, and then we all stared at each other.

"Well, since I asked you to come, I'll start. I wanted to tell you that I was sorry, Beka. If I could take it all back, I would. And I guess I owe you an apology too, Lori. I never even gave you a chance."

Lori narrowed her eyes for a minute, then whispered, "I forgive you."

"And I already told you that I forgive you," I said.

"I know." Gretchen stirred her soda when the waitress placed it in front of her. "Can I see it?"

I lifted my eyebrows. "See what?"

"Where they hurt you."

I glanced at Lori, who shrugged. I lifted up a corner of my shirt, and Gretchen leaned over the table to see the four-inch-long scar on my abdomen.

She sat back, and the cushion whined as the air was forced back out of it. "You weren't supposed to get hurt. I never meant for that to happen."

"I know."

Gretchen's expression was different than anything I had seen on her face before. She told us about her new school and that she had a new boyfriend, a nice one this time, and how she was trying to get her life back together.

"I needed a fresh start," she said when she told us about the transfer. "I just couldn't go back to all of that."

"It's just as well. Mai has been just so much fun to deal with since you've been gone," I said.

"I could give you some dirt on her. She'd probably leave you alone."

It was a tempting thought, but even as it flitted across my mind, I knew I wouldn't play dirty.

"No. It'll be fine."

Gretchen shook her head. "You've really changed a lot, Beka. I mean that in a good way. I just don't get it."

"It's God, Gretchen, not me."

She rolled her eyes. "Yeah, you talked a lot about that at the hospital."

"You heard me?" I felt the soda tickle my nose as I struggled to swallow it.

"Sort of. It's all kind of hazy, almost like it was a dream, but I heard your voice, and I remember some of what I assumed you said." She crumpled the straw wrapper between two fingers. "You were the only one who came to visit."

"Your mom told me."

"My mom." Gretchen snorted. "She walks around me like I'm going to explode at any moment. But I'm better. I guess I thought everything was over. All my plans. Everything."

"And now?"

"Now I'll go to the community college for a year or two, then try to transfer. I still want to go to New York."

We talked for a while longer, but then we said our good-byes. She didn't bring up God again, and neither did we. If she wanted to talk about it, she could have. But it seemed like just by forgiving her, I had made an impact on her.

It felt good.

I still didn't know how to help Lori, though, and she looked sadder than ever on the drive back to my house. Being there just didn't seem like enough to me.

*   *   *

"You're really applying to Seattle Pacific? You keep saying you're just friends with him," Lori said.

"I am."

"Sure. I'm glad you're applying to Tech. I think that's my first choice."

"Oh, and I'm sure that has nothing to do with Brian being there, right?" I teased.

"No, not at all." She laughed. "It is a great school

though, and with in-state tuition it won't be too bad for my mom, even if . . ." Her face clouded over.

"Well, I have to apply to five, so I'm doing Seattle, Tech, this liberal arts one, and these two Christian ones. That's the one my brother goes to." I pointed at the top brochure and handed them to her.

She flipped through them. "Which one do you want to get into?"

"Is it crazy to say that I don't really care? It's weird. I guess I just want to go to college. I'm supposed to go."

"If you could do anything, though, what would it be? If you could choose it and you were guaranteed to get what you want, what would you choose?"

"This music theory class I'm taking is so great. Even though I have to see Mark in it every day. It's hard, but I really like it. Maybe I could get good at it and teach music or something."

"Speaking of music, are you going to play your song for me yet?"

"It's not finished."

"So music, huh?"

"Yeah. It's the thing I like the most. Lots of kids started playing when they were really little. I feel like I got a late start."

"I doubt that will matter. If you're supposed to do it, then you'll be able to learn all that you have to."

"I still have to play at the holiday concert." I took a deep breath. "I'm so nervous. I've only played in class and at the Bible school in Haiti. And they didn't care what I sounded like."

We went to bed, and I had a terrible dream of being on stage at the concert, and all my guitar strings snapped, and Mai was making the whole school laugh at me. As if I wasn't worried enough.

*   *   *

Janne agreed to help me after school during the last week before break. The concert was scheduled for Saturday night, so every day we holed up in a practice room. Mark's practice room.

On Friday, I dragged myself to the music wing after journalism class, feeling tired and cranky and ready for a break. I didn't even look before I opened the door, and I walked in on Mark playing. He looked at me and smiled that smile.

I felt like I was trying to stop an ice cube from melting as my heart made a puddle in my chest.

"Sorry. I'll wait till you're done." I closed the door and went and sat against the wall across the hall. Why did he have that effect on me? I drummed my fingers on my guitar case as I tried to list the reasons I was better off without him.

I couldn't even come up with one.

A few minutes later he came out with his case in his hand and stood looking down at me with a half smile on his face.

"How's your song coming?" he asked.

"Good, I think. Janne's helping me."

"I know."

The silence thickened between us.

"So when do you finish?"

"By four. Why?"

"I just thought we could go get a coffee or something."

"Again? Why?"

"To talk. Catch up." He crouched down and put his hand on my leg. "I miss you."

"Oh, really. Could have fooled me."

Mark rolled his eyes. "Look, can we talk about this later?"

"Sure. Janne's here anyway." I stood up, and Mark caught my hand.

"Will you meet me? At the beach."

"It's freezing outside. What about The Fire Escape?"

"Got it. Four thirty okay?"

I nodded and watched him walk down the hallway.

I went into the practice room and opened my case. Janne was already tuning his guitar.

"Our last day to practice," he said.

"I know. Do you think it will be okay?"

"Song is beautiful. It will be great."

Janne was helping me and another group with arranging the music, so his grade depended partially on how I did. Which made me twice as nervous.

After we practiced, I drove to The Fire Escape wondering if I should be meeting Mark at all. I wanted to. But I felt like the entire time I had known him I was just reacting to him. If he drew close to me, I let him; if he pulled away, I watched him go.

And I was mad at him for doing that to me. I pulled into the parking lot, turned the car off, and closed my eyes. I knew I needed to forgive him, but when it came to someone like Mark, it just seemed more complicated.

I prayed for him and myself and for God to forgive me for being angry with him, but I still didn't know how to act when I went inside.

He was sitting at the corner table, and he lifted his hand as I walked to him. He smiled. I pulled out the heavy chair, and it squeaked across the floor. I cringed and sat down.

"You hungry?" he asked.

"I'll just get a soda."

Mark ordered our drinks and some nachos for us. Once we had our drinks he watched me until I cleared my throat.

"So why am I here, Mark? You're dating someone else."

"Who, Angela? Where'd you hear that?"

"Where didn't I hear it? Somehow, the ex, if I even qualify for that, always gets to hear those details."

"Angela and I aren't serious. We've only been out a few times."

"Why am I here, Mark?"

"I told you; I miss you."

"Mark. This isn't going to work."

"What?"

"This. You don't want to be serious, and I'm not willing to be part of a harem."

"So that's it? You don't even want to try?"

"What does that mean to you, exactly?"

"Go out with me." He reached across the small table and took my hand.

"Why now, Mark?"

He sighed. "There's just no one like you. Angela's nice, but she's not you."

"Are you going to keep seeing her? Or someone else?"

"Let's just agree to try again. See where it goes."

"Mark. You're going to have to do better than that for me. I'm worth more than that." I stood up. "See ya tomorrow."

I walked away, and once again the thought crossed my mind, *Will he come after me?* I got to my car and climbed in. It didn't feel like a mistake though. It was my last year of high school. Everything would change next year anyway. Right?

He didn't come after me.

I looked at my watch and sighed. I was supposed to pick up Lucy and Anna, and I was supposed to get the three of us to The Greens, a fancy restaurant outside of town, to meet Dad and Gabby and her relatives. I had less than an hour to get there. I didn't have time to worry about Mark.

I could do that later.

*   *   *

"C'mon, Luce. Let's go." I twisted Anna's hair up into a French twist and started poking bobby pins into it.

"Why do I have to get all dressed up?" Anna pulled at her tights.

I pulled her upright. "Stay still so I can do this. Lucy! It's an expensive restaurant. We're supposed to look nice."

Lucy came down the stairs dressed in a blouse and skirt, her hair clipped back with jeweled barrettes.

"Can you find Anna's shoes?" She nodded, and I let go of Anna's hair to see if I had it all pinned down. I pushed at it and pulled one piece tighter, poking one last bobby pin into it.

"We're ready." I ran to the bathroom as quickly as I could in my heels and checked my face. I had twisted my hair up too, and it looked nice, but I still wanted to change it. Maybe it was time to do it. Before I had to go onstage tomorrow. A new me.

"Let's go!" I said as I grabbed my purse and car keys.

We piled into the car and made it to the restaurant with three minutes to spare. Even with the cold air blowing I felt hot from all the running around. And because of what lay ahead.

Gabby's brother and his wife were in town for the holidays, and Dad wanted us all to get together. I asked if we could wait until after my concert, but he insisted on taking them all out their first night in town. He was going to a lot of trouble. That could be pointing only in one direction.

I had been getting along with Gabby a lot better. I was even starting to enjoy being with her. But it still felt weird to think that she could become my stepmother.

I took Anna's hand. We walked into the restaurant together, and we were taken to a private dining room. My dad stood up as we walked in.

"My beautiful girls. Wow." He hugged each of us, and when he hugged me he whispered "Thank you" in my ear.

Gabby came over, followed by a beautiful brunette who looked to be Mexican and a tall man with a goatee and a jacket. They looked like they were straight off the red carpet.

"Girls, I want you to meet my big brother, Tony, and his wife, Carlita. This is Anna, Lucy, and Beka." We all shook hands with Tony, but Carlita hugged us all.

"We've heard so much about you," she gushed.

"It's great to finally meet the family Gabby's been talking about," Tony said as he hooked his arm around Gabby's neck and squeezed. She smiled up at him.

We all moved to the table, and after the ordering was done the adults talked about the record company that Tony owned with his best friend in California and Carlita's job at Paramount Studios as a creative producer. I had no idea what that meant, but they dropped names of stars that I had only seen on TV and in the movies.

Their lives sounded so glamorous. I found myself so enthralled with their stories that I was caught off guard when Gabby pointed at me.

Beka's performing tomorrow night. She won't let anyone hear her song, but she's got a beautiful voice," Gabby said.

"Really? I'd love to see that." Tony and Carlita spoke over each other.

"Oh." I wiped my mouth with the linen napkin. "It's just a little high school concert. It's nothing like what you're used to."

"Don't worry, Tony. I already bought tickets. We're all going," Gabby said.

I tried to swallow the food that felt caught in my throat.

"Great. What do you play, Beka?" Tony asked.

"The guitar. I just started though. I'm not really very good."

"So tell me about this concert," he said.

The whole table focused on me. The only sound was the forks scraping the plates.

"Umm. Well, it's the whole music department. The show band will be playing, and I think the choir is singing, and then there's what I'm a part of."

Tony jutted his chin forward, urging me to continue.

"Well, I take a music theory class, and we had to do a semester project. I chose to write a song. I have someone helping me with the composition, but the lyrics are mine."

"How old are you?"

"Seventeen."

"Well, I can't wait to hear it."

I was relieved when my dad asked another question and the conversation shifted again. Carlita asked about Lucy's gymnastics and Anna's riding, and I was surprised they seemed so interested in all of it. Our lives seemed very plain in comparison to theirs.

The dinner went on for a long time, and Anna was yawning by the time dessert came. I really liked Gabby's brother and sister-in-law, and I got to see a different side of her—the little sister side. It made me miss my own big brother, and I was so glad Paul was coming home tomorrow.

*   *   *

When we got back, I helped Anna take her hair down, and Dad tucked her into bed and kissed Lucy good night. I was flipping channels on the TV when he came back down.

He sank into his recliner and sighed.

"So what did you think?"

"They're great. Did you see her dress? It looked like something they would wear to an awards show, didn't it?"

"I guess. Not my department."

"And he's so cool. I can't believe he knows all those famous singers."

Dad laughed. "I'm glad you like them." His face grew serious.

"What's wrong?"

Dad leaned forward and rubbed his hands together. "Well, there's something I wanted to talk to you about."

I muted the television and watched him.

"You seem to be doing better with Gabby lately, but we haven't talked a lot about it."

"Yeah. It's okay. I guess I'm getting used to the idea."

"Well." He coughed and cleared his throat. "How would you feel if I . . . well . . . if I asked Gabby to . . . um, marry me?"

Even though I knew the question would come, it still took my breath away. He was serious. He wanted to marry someone. He wanted to marry her.

"You see, well, I want to talk to each of you separately about it. So you could ask questions. Anything. I want to know how you feel about it."

I fought to make all the thoughts running through my mind settle down so I could think.

He cleared his throat again. "I know it seems quick,

but I've been praying about this for a long time. The fact is, your mom wanted me to get married again if something happened to her, and I just didn't think I'd ever want to. But this—this surprised me. God surprised me. You know, there's four of you kids, and each time your mom got pregnant I thought, *There's no way I can love this new one as much as I love the ones I already have.* But it was never a matter of loving more or less; it was like my love just grew bigger. Like a whole new room of my heart opened up every time. And it surprised me each time."

He looked at me, then stood and paced on the floor in front of me. I still was trying to decide what to say.

"That's what this is like. I don't love Gabby more than your mother or less than your mother. Mom will always have a whole room of my heart that will never belong to anyone else again." He stopped and looked up for a moment and squeezed the bridge of his nose. "God has just opened up a different room. For Gabby. Does that make sense?"

"I guess."

He came over and knelt down in front of me. "Tell me how you feel. I want to know."

"So you're in love with her?"

He nodded. "Yes, but like I said, it's just a new part of my heart."

"It's just so fast. You've only been dating, what, a few months."

"I know. But I've been meeting with Pastor Mark about this. I feel like this is something God has done, and when He does things, it's just right."

"When?"

"The spring, maybe. But I'd like to ask her this Christmas. With all of you there. What do you think?"

I thought through the sentence before I said it. "If it will make you happy, then it will make me happy."

Dad collapsed on me and hugged me tight. When he pulled back there were tears in his eyes.

"I love you, Dad. I really do."

He blew out his breath and then smiled. "That was harder than I thought it would be."

"Have you talked to the others yet?"

"No. I tackled you first." He poked me in the ribs to tickle me. "I figured if I could get through you, everybody else will be a breeze. But don't tell anyone until I talk to them, okay?"

I turned my fingers against my lips and lifted my hand, vowing to say nothing.

Dad brushed my hair out of my face. "Your mom would be so proud of you. You know that, don't you?"

I nodded.

"How are the applications coming?" he asked, standing up and moving back to his recliner.

I rolled my eyes. "Slow. I still have no clue where I should go. Or where God wants me to go. Do you really think there's a right school for me?"

"Absolutely. I don't think He has a plan for part of our lives, and no plan for other parts. He's got a plan, and it's always better than the one we've made."

"What if we have no idea?"

"Then fill out the applications, send them in, and wait for the answers. Sometimes we're being led by God and we don't even know it."

I went to bed imagining what it would be like to watch Dad get married. I had seen the video of when he married Mom, both of them looking like young kids, with love filling their eyes. But this time I would be there.

I meant what I had said to my dad, but I still cried myself to sleep, wishing that life had never taken such a drastic turn. Wondering where I would be if I had another chance with Mom.

*   *   *

I woke up early, feeling like I had never really gotten to sleep.

The concert wasn't for twelve hours, but it was the first thought that popped into my head. I crawled out of bed, took my guitar, and crawled back into bed with it. I strummed it, my fingers moving through the chords almost without thinking. The trick would be to do it while I was sitting onstage.

*   *   *

By noon we were all pacing around the kitchen, waiting for Paul to arrive. I made some grilled cheese sandwiches to keep myself busy. Dad had already taken Lucy aside, and he gave me a thumbs-up when he got back. He was going to save Anna till last, because she just couldn't keep a secret.

Paul finally got home, and after the hugs and un-loading, we spent the afternoon as a family decorating the tree in the living room. It struck me halfway through that if Gabby and Dad got married, there would be someone else in on this tradition.

Paul told us about school and his classes and how he would be gearing up for baseball as soon as he returned to school. It was a great day. Once we finished the decorating, Dad took Paul out to talk to him, and Lucy shot me a knowing look.

"Could you stay with Anna till Dad gets back?" I asked Lucy. "I'm going to get my hair cut."

"I guess."

"Thanks. And I'm going straight over to the school to be there for the sound checks, so let Dad know, okay?"

Lucy waved her hand at me, and I went to get all my stuff together, my guitar and the skirt and sweater I was going to wear, and jumped in my car. I drove to the salon considering my options. I didn't know if I was ready for anything drastic, and by the time I was in the chair I was having serious second thoughts.

"So what are we going to do today?" Vicki asked, lifting my hair and letting it fall through her fingers.

"I don't know. Something different?"

She smacked her gum and shifted her hip. "Honey, now don't you do anything you don't want to do." She dropped her ear to her shoulder and looked in the mirror. "Why don't we taper the sides a bit, take a little off the length, and put some long layers in to give it a bit more body?"

"Okay." I sat back and let her start snipping away. I ran through my song in my head even though I knew it cold. It was only going to be three minutes. Why was I so nervous?

Vicki blow-dried my hair. "See, that frames your face beautifully."

I looked in the mirror and smiled. It wasn't drastic, but it made a big difference. It felt pretty and soft around my face. I paid for the haircut and waved good-bye to Vicki, my new favorite person.

*   *   *

I decided to wait until after sound checks to change into my clothes. My big decision at that point was stool or no stool. I was very glad I was playing the guitar, because I wouldn't have known what to do with my hands otherwise.

They went through the program in order. The performance projects were sprinkled throughout the evening, in between the chorus and the show band, and I was the last one to go before the brief intermission. I was going to have to wait through half the concert.

I sang and played through the song while they checked everything, and I used the time to double-check the tuning. Once they finished with me, I went back to the band room and found a spot to sit and wait.

I leaned back, closed my eyes, and prayed. I'd like to say that I prayed for the ills of the world and for people I cared about, but I pretty much asked God to not let me mess up. Just get me through the song.

"So. You're all ready?"

Even before I opened my eyes I knew Mark was standing in front of me.

"Not yet. I still have to change."

Mark wrote on the clipboard he was carrying. "But your sound checks are done?"

I nodded and looked into his eyes. Why couldn't things be different? If I went by his terms I could be with him.

"Beka."

"What?"

He paused. "Never mind. Do great tonight."

"Thanks." He walked away, and part of me wanted to jump up and go after him this time. But I just sat.

I went and got changed and wandered up to the lobby to see my family.

"Love the hair!" Gabby said when I spotted them by the concession table.

"You didn't say anything about getting a haircut," Dad said. "I like it though."

"Hi Tony, Carlita," I said. Carlita gave me a hug, and Tony handed me a big bouquet of flowers.

"From all of us," he said.

"Thanks." Tony squeezed my shoulder.

"It's so strange being back here." Paul laughed. "College makes everything seem so much smaller."

"Well, I better get backstage. Thanks for coming. All of you."

"We wouldn't have missed it," Dad said.

I walked across the foyer that was starting to fill up and saw Nancy coming in the door. I went over to her.

"Hey. You came," I said.

"Sure. I've been praying for your song for a month now. I had to at least hear it." Nancy laughed and then smiled. "Josh is parking the car."

"Josh is here?" My chest tightened.

She nodded. "He got home yesterday, but when I told him about this he said he wanted to wait until tonight to let you know."

I breathed slow and deep to calm myself.

"I guess I didn't know . . . I didn't think . . ." Josh, bundled up in a mocha brown jacket, pulled open the door behind Nancy.

He was carrying roses.

"Beka. You're here!"

"Right back at ya."

Josh looked at Nancy and then back at me. "These are for you." He handed me the flowers.

"You didn't have to do that. Thanks." I looked at the pink sweetheart roses nestled in the bright green paper.

"I'm going to get a soda. Want anything, Josh?" Nancy asked.

Josh shook his head, and Nancy moved away. I looked him over. He seemed older than when he left.

"You changed your hair," he said after a minute. Mark hadn't even noticed that. "I like it."

I reached up and touched it. "It was impulsive. I needed a change."

"It's good to see you. I didn't call yesterday because I thought, well, I didn't want to make you more nervous. I was going to come backstage after."

"I'm glad you came. Really." My heart skittered around inside my chest.

"Do you think we could go out after the concert, just get a soda or a coffee? For a little while?"

"Umm, probably. I'll check with my dad. I really have to go now though."

"Go ahead. I'll go find Nancy."

I turned to leave, and he grabbed my elbow and pulled me into a hug.

"I've missed you," he whispered in my ear.

"Me too."

I pulled away only because I began to imagine Thompson turning redder by the second.

"I have to go."

I sprinted down the hallway and reached the stage door just as Thompson said, "Okay, people. Let's get ready."

CHAPTER 24

I paced around the hallway as the first act was ushered through the double doors and out onto the stage.

"Beka!" Lori came from around the corner. She took a second to catch her breath. "I'm glad you weren't first!" She laughed and hugged me.

"I'm so glad you're here. Can you stay?"

Lori nodded. "Mom and Kari Lynn are out front."

"No David?"

She shook her head. "Have faith, right?"

"Right."

Lori and I sat in the hallway as each act went onstage and then came out, letting the applause filter back to where we were sitting. Mark came out the stage doors and looked around.

"Beka. You ready?"

I stood up and smoothed out my skirt and shirt. "Do I look okay?" I asked Lori.

"Perfect," she said.

We walked up to Mark. "She's watching from the wings." I pointed my thumb at Lori.

We followed him into the darkness, and when the applause began for Kris's band, Mark walked me out onstage. He and Janne set the guitar and voice mikes in front of me and repositioned the monitor so I could hear. Mark handed me my guitar, and I slipped the strap over my head.

I suddenly wished I had asked for a stool. My legs felt like they were going to wilt right underneath me. With the spotlights, I couldn't see anybody in the audience.

I wrapped my fingers around the neck of the guitar and squeezed, feeling nothing but a lump in my throat. *Lord, I need some help.* I closed my eyes and took a deep breath, careful not to blow into the microphone in front of me.

I picked up my hand and strummed the first chords. The words came right when they were supposed to.

You Found Me

From a lie, I was born.
From the darkness I traveled
To the light of the morning sun.

Down a long road I walked,
Through a forest of faces.
Searching only for something real.

Then You came to me
And saved me from myself.

You came and found me.
Picked me up off the ground,
Turned my world upside down.
You found me.
I can't thank you enough
For Your unending love.

I was close to the edge
When You came to my rescue.
Held me tight and never let me go.

You came to me,
Salvation in Your hand.

When things get too hard
I trust that You'll look down and see me.
And when I feel scared
I know You will come and free me.

I struck the last chord, and the music faded and then
stopped. A long pause. Was it awful?
Then the crowd broke into applause, loud and long.
The houselights came up for the intermission, and I saw

the crowd on their feet as the curtain closed in front of me. Lori came running out and hugged me.

"You're amazing! You wrote that?"

"Umm, Janne helped me."

"Wow." She shook her head. "I definitely agree that music is where you belong, no matter what you end up doing."

Lori and I went to the back of the stage, where I ran into Thompson. "You just got yourself an A," he said.

Lori and I found a spot in the wings where we could listen to the rest of the concert. But I barely heard any of it. I kept reliving my three minutes onstage. It was amazing. All the nervous jitters flew away as soon as I started playing. It all felt so right.

When the concert ended, we all went back onstage for a final bow. I spent a few minutes congratulating my classmates. Mark found me in the throng.

"You always surprise me, Beka."

"I surprised myself. I didn't think I was going to be able to do it."

Mark stepped close, just a breath away. "You looked so beautiful out there."

I watched him as he searched my face and eyes. I didn't know what to say.

"Um, thanks, Mark." I turned away, and he slipped his hand into mine, pulling me close again.

"I need you in my life, Beka."

"Mark. You can't keep doing this to me. It hurts."

"I'm a guy, Beka. I make mistakes."

"I have to go see my family."

"Then meet me later."

"I can't, Mark. I have plans."

"So change them." His lips were so close now that I thought he was going to kiss me.

I pulled away. "I won't change them. You're the one that keeps changing your mind. Not me."

I packed up my guitar and found Dad in the hallway.

"Beka!" He wrapped his arms around me. "God has really blessed you, hasn't He?"

"Dad, I know Tony and Carlita are coming over, but . . . well, Josh is home."

"Be back by midnight," he said.

"Thanks." I hugged him again and went to find Josh. Lori had already left, making me promise I would call her on Sunday to tell her how it went. She wasn't going to believe what Mark had said either.

Josh and Nancy were waiting by the door.

"Beka, that was wonderful. Such a beautiful song." They spoke at the same time.

Josh reached down and took my guitar. "Can we take your car so Nancy can drive home?" he asked.

"Sure."

We said good-bye to Nancy, who gave me a wink before we left. It helped that she was okay with Josh and me going out, but I still wasn't sure what it was. Was it a real date? And all those letters he had written. I was so unsure what he meant by them.

We agreed to go to The Fire Escape, and we drove there in silence. We sat at a table and ordered drinks.

I was sure he could hear my heart thumping.

What was I supposed to say?

"I can't believe I'm really here," he said.

"It seems like you've been gone forever."

"I'm glad you could come out tonight, but I'd still like to see you again before I leave. Take you to a nice dinner, a movie, or something."

I swallowed. "I'd like that."

He lives three thousand miles away. What am I doing?

I took a long drink out of my straw and looked around the place. Mai came in with several friends, including Liz.

"Great."

Josh looked where I was looking. "Friends of yours?" he asked.

"Not the word I would use." I told him about Mai and what had happened with Gretchen and the assembly.

"You've been busy." He smiled at me. "You didn't mention any of that in your letters."

"I know. I wasn't sure . . . I didn't want to bore you with all my high school dramas."

"I want to hear it, though. It's not boring."

"I'm not used to writing letters, I guess." I stirred the ice in my soda.

"Well, you're quite a songwriter. You blew me away."

I could feel the heat rising up my neck. "I had help."

Josh looked around and leaned forward on his arm. "So, do you know what you're going to be when you grow up yet?"

"Something with music, I suppose. It was so much fun to work on that song. I have a lot to learn, but it seems right."

"God has given you an amazing gift." He looked deep into my eyes, making me tense again. "I bet you'd love Seattle."

I weighed my words. Should I tell him I had filled out the application? It would make it obvious that I cared about him, if it wasn't obvious already. But it was such a long shot. I hadn't even told my dad that was one of the schools I was applying to.

He must have read my hesitation. "I'm sorry. I don't want to pressure you or anything." He lifted his hands in the air. "I just hate being so far away from you. I've wanted to go to Seattle for years, but now all I can think about is how far away it is."

I chewed on my lower lip, trying to understand what he wasn't saying.

The moment passed, and we moved on to talk about his classes and my last semester of school. I drove him home, and when we pulled in the driveway he picked up my hand and kissed it.

"So, we'll get together next week. Right?"

"Yeah."

I watched him walk to his door, and before he went in he turned around and waved. I drove home slowly, my thoughts about Mark and Josh too confused to sort themselves out. When I got home I saw Gabby's truck and what must have been Tony and Carlita's rental in the driveway. I wasn't in the mood to chat. I really wanted to just think. Maybe pray.

*　　*　　*

I found everyone in the living room and was greeted with a round of applause. I smiled and covered my mouth.

"Beka, come in and sit for a few minutes," Dad said.

I came in and sat on the ottoman, the only seat left in the room.

They all looked at each other, as if they were trying to decide who was going to talk first.

"What? Is something wrong?" I asked.

"No, no, no. It's just . . . Well, Tony?" Dad looked at Tony, who was sitting on the couch with his arm around Carlita.

Tony sat forward and slapped his hands together. "Your song. Fabulous. I was talking with your dad about getting a demo recorded so I have something to take back to L.A. and show to my board."

"What?"

Gabby jumped in. "He wants you to record your song so that he can try to get you a recording contract." She was almost squealing.

I looked around at each of them. They stared at me, waiting for some reaction.

"But I'm not . . . I mean . . . I just started. Dad?"

Dad laced his fingers together. "What do you think, Butterfly?"

I had nothing. My mind felt stunned into blankness.

Tony spoke up. "No need to get panicked. Let's just do the demo. See what happens. I run the company with a friend, and we have a board that helps decide on new artists. If it were up to me, I'd sign you now, but it's not."

"Like sing my song in a studio? With those earphones and stuff like you see on the 'Making of . . .' video specials?"

Tony and Carlita grinned. "Yeah, like that. Your dad said he would leave it up to you."

I looked back at Dad.

"It wouldn't hurt to do the demo. It might be nice for you to have it anyway."

"Okay."

Tony slapped his hands together. "Great, then I'll get something lined up before we leave. We have to get it done before Christmas though. Excuse me—I have to make a few calls." He flipped open his phone and kissed Carlita before he left the room.

"This is so exciting. I mean, I thought he would like you, but I wasn't expecting this," Gabby said.

"A demo?" I said the words, hoping it would make it seem real. "Carlita. What if they like the demo at Tony's studio? What would happen?"

"Well. They would offer you a contract to record a CD. They'd pay you. You'd have to live in L.A. though, at least during the recording."

"L.A.?"

"Yes. But you could stay with us. We have no children and a house bigger than we need. It would be fun to have you." She smiled. "Don't worry, Beka. Take it one step at a time. Okay?"

I nodded, a feeling of excitement starting to form inside. Could I hear my very own song on the radio someday?

*   *   *

It was impossible to sleep. It was too late to call Lori, so I just ran over the whole night in my head until I was too tired to think. And still I couldn't sleep. I had learned that God had a plan for everyone, but this kind of plan had never even entered my thoughts. Was God doing this? And if He was, what would it do to my quiet little suburban life, where my biggest worry was over a couple of guys?

And how would I know if it was Him making all this happen?

I don't want anyone to know about

it, so don't tell anyone." I had called Lori to tell her about
Tony's offer the next day.

"Why not? That is, like, the most exciting thing that's
ever happened to anybody I've ever known."

"It is pretty cool, isn't it? We've only got three more
days of school anyway, and then it's off for Christmas. I'd
rather wait to see if anything happens. Tony's business
partners may not like it as much."

"Don't worry, Beka. God started this, and He's going
to finish it."

"So you think God's doing it? Really?"

"Beka, think about everything God put in place to

get you to this point. And it's not just the guitar lessons, but your class, the concert, and Gabby having a brother who just happens to be a record producer and happened to be in town to hear the concert? Come on."

"You're right. It's just so unbelievable. Isn't it?"

"But way cool."

*   *   *

Tony scheduled the demo recording for Wednesday afternoon, right after school let out for winter break. It seemed like the last three days took forever. Mai was pretty much ignoring me, which I didn't have a problem with, though she did make one rude comment about seeing Josh and me at The Fire Escape. Lori went back and forth between being happy for me and sad about her family and the holidays. And Mark. He was following me around again.

He plopped into the seat next to mine in music theory.

"What?" I asked.

"Nothing."

I looked over at him. He was slouched in his chair with his hands folded across his stomach. I let one laugh escape. He looked awfully cute sitting there pouting.

"You pushed me away. Remember?" I said.

"I don't remember anything like that."

"Mark, you're more confused than I am, and that's saying a lot."

"Maybe I was upset. But I wasn't expecting you to listen to me."

"So you expected me to grovel for you?"

"Grovel? No. But some sort of protest, at least."

"I don't play games, Mark. Maybe some girls do, but not this girl," I said.

He stared at the ceiling for a minute, and I chewed on the end of my pencil. Then he shot upright in his chair and took my hand in both of his. "So what then? What do I need to do?"

"You don't have to do anything. You made it very clear what you wanted, and that's not what I want."

"Why do you have to make me work so hard?" He sighed.

Another laugh escaped. And why couldn't I just tell him to go away?

I got this urge to tell him about the demo, but I resisted. What if it didn't work out?

"You know we're going to end up together, right?" He looked at me and batted his eyes.

"Says who?"

He shrugged. "I'm just meant to love you."

I let the comment slide past and instead focused on the fact that there were only a couple of hours left before I cut my first demo. I shook my head. I never would have believed that I would think such a thing.

*   *   *

I really thought it was Tony who was going to come pick Lori and me up for the recording. But while we were standing in the kitchen watching the driveway, a white stretch limo pulled in.

"Is that for me?" I stared openmouthed at it.

Lori squealed. "It's like you're already a star!"

We went out, and after the driver assured me that he was there for us we piled in and, despite the temperature outside, opened the sunroof.

"Could you imagine living like this?" Lori lay back on the leather seats.

"Not at all."

The studio was almost an hour away, because Tony insisted on finding one that had top-of-the-line equipment. We went in, and Tony greeted us in the small waiting room.

"There's my girl," he said.

I smiled as he put his arm around me and led me to another room that had glass all along one wall. I could see two men and a woman in the booth behind the glass. They raised their hands at me for a second before they went back to work.

Lori looked at me and grinned.

I tried to take in the whole experience, but there was so much going on that I felt like I was mostly just following directions. Sing this part. Play this part. Let's try that one again. Three hours later Tony was happy with the song, and he walked us back out to the limo.

"I have to tell you, the limo was a surprise," I said.

"I would have done it for someone in L.A.; why not you?"

"Well, thanks for going to all this trouble. This was great," I said.

"Hey, now. I'm making an investment in you. It's no trouble, because I'm expecting great things from you." He lifted my chin with his hand.

I hardly knew whether he was serious or not. Maybe everybody in L.A. talked like that. They certainly didn't talk like that in suburbia.

Now the waiting would begin.

Tony warned me that the decision process was long and that I should continue my plans. Which meant mailing those college applications that I had finally completed. Dad didn't say anything when he wrote the check to Seattle Pacific. I took that as a good sign.

But I wondered. Where would I be next year?

College?

Or L.A.?

On Christmas Day, Dad popped

the question. He did it in front of all of us, on his knees, and he gave her a gorgeous diamond ring. Gabby cried a river and eagerly said yes at least a dozen times.

They looked happy. I tried to be. But in that room, surrounded by the Christmas tree and the decorations and the music, I could almost feel Mom there. It didn't seem wrong, but it didn't feel right either.

Missing her was just a way of life now. And maybe that's the way I would always feel. I wasn't too sure.

I saw Josh twice over the holidays. Each time it was weird and wonderful. Wonderful because I felt myself melting toward him again in the way he looked at me and spoke to me, but weird because it felt like there was so much more that needed to be said and neither of us said it. He went back to school, and still I wasn't sure what to call the relationship. Were we more than friends, or not?

Mark called twice, but both times I was out. I decided to let him sweat it out and not call back right away. I would see him in school soon enough.

I still wasn't sure what God thought of the whole thing, but I needed to find out.

One thing that I knew was sorely lacking in my life was knowing how to really study the Bible. Even though things were tough at her house, Lori's mom agreed to meet with us, and this time I was determined to make it work. With the wedding set for the spring, and the boy situation, I felt like I needed to understand a lot more than I did.

*　　　*　　　*

On New Year's Day I bundled up and went to sit at the foot of Mom's grave, looking at the script that read, "Beloved Wife and Mother." I told her about everything, but mostly I talked about Gabby.

Make room.

I didn't want to make room. I wanted my mother back.

Make room.

I folded my legs up and wrapped my arms around them. Would it ever be different? Would the ache ever go away?

I watched the sun set through the trees just past her grave, the sky moving from gray to brilliant color.

Maybe that's what life was like—the grays giving way to color when the time was right. Was it okay to enjoy all that was happening?

The wind blew, biting my cheeks with the cold.

Could I just be happy again? Without guilt?

Make room.

It wasn't just Gabby I needed to make room for, but also joy and expectation, peace, and a bit of love too.

I sat there until the darkness fell.

Wish you were here.

Want to hear Beka's song?

Visit
www.becomingbeka.com

You can download Beka's song!

You'll also find:

Fun quizzes
Free stuff
Info and help
Contests
And much more

Congratulations to our character winner,
Caitie Karraker, and to the top five runners-up:
Anna B., Krista S., Brittany H., Jordan B., and Kecia L.

Check the Web site for future contests!

The Becoming Beka series

Beka has been trying to move on with her life since her mother's tragic accident, but it feels like she's going nowhere fast. Things are not so good at home. Beka's brother and sisters won't leave her alone. Her scary dreams keep coming back. And worst of all, Beka has a secret she can't share with anyone, especially not her family.

The Masquerade
ISBN: 0-8024-6451-3
ISBN-13: 978-0-8024-6451-4

When Beka heads back to school with a newfound faith, she expects some special feeling, some enlightenment, something different. But what she feels is . . . nothing. In fact, what she faces is a series of tough choices. For some reason Gretchen, the most powerful and popular girl in school, takes an interest in Beka, and Beka finds herself enjoying the popularity. But Gretchen's attention comes with a price.

The Alliance
ISBN: 0-8024-6452-1
ISBN-13: 978-0-8024-6452-1

Life can be confusing. Especially when it comes to boys. As Beka's junior year winds to a close, Josh and Mark are both vying for her affections. Since Josh is going to college in Seattle in the fall it seems clear that Mark, a fellow junior, is her best chance for finally having a boyfriend. But with her dad's strict rules about spending time with guys, Beka's left frustrated and wondering if she'll ever have a boyfriend.

The Passage
ISBN: 0-8024-6453-X
ISBN-13: 978-0-8024-6453-8

S INCE 1894, Moody Publishers has been dedicated to equip and motivate people to advance the cause of Christ by publishing evangelical Christian literature and other media for all ages, around the world. Because we are a ministry of the Moody Bible Institute of Chicago, a portion of the proceeds from the sale of this book go to train the next generation of Christian leaders.

If we may serve you in any way in your spiritual journey toward understanding Christ and the Christian life, please contact us at www.moodypublishers.com.

MOODY
PUBLISHERS

THE NAME YOU CAN TRUST®

THE REVEAL TEAM

ACQUIRING EDITOR
Andy McGuire

BACK COVER COPY
Lisa Ann Cockrel

COPY EDITOR
Cheryl Dunlop

COVER DESIGN
LeVan Fisher Design

COVER PHOTO
Steve Gardner, www.pixelworksstudio.net

INTERIOR DESIGN
Ragont Design

PRINTING AND BINDING
Bethany Press International

The typeface for the text of this book is
Aetna JY